KING OF ROGUES

A Rogues of the Road novel

SASHA COTTMAN

Also by Sasha Cottman

SERIES

The Duke of Strathmore

The Noble Lords

Rogues of the Road

London Lords

For other releases visit www.sashacottman.com

The Duke of Strathmore

Letter from a Rake – eBook, Audio, Print

An Unsuitable Match – eBook, Audio, Print

The Duke's Daughter – eBook, Audio, Print

A Scottish Duke for Christmas – eBook, Print

My Gentleman Spy – eBook, Audio, Print

Lord of Mischief – eBook, Audio, Print

The Ice Queen – eBook, Audio, Print

Two of a Kind – eBook, Audio, Print

A Lady's Heart Deceived - eBook, Print

Mistletoe and Kisses (novella) – eBook, Print

A Wild English Rose – exclusive eBook, Print

The Noble Lords

Love Lessons for the Viscount – eBook, Print

A Lord with Wicked Intentions – eBook, Print

A Scandalous Rogue for Lady Eliza – eBook, Print

Unexpected Duke– eBook, Print

The Noble Lords Boxed Set

Rogues of the Road

Rogue for Hire – eBook, Print

Stolen by the Rogue – eBook, Print

When a Rogue Falls – eBook, Print

The Rogue and the Jewel – eBook, Print

King of Rogues – eBook, Print

London Lords

Devoted to the Spanish Duke – eBook, Print

Promised to the Swedish Prince – eBook, Print

An Italian Count for Christmas – eBook, Print

Wedded to the Welsh Baron – eBook, Print

Bound to the Belgian Count – eBook, Print

Join my VIP readers for your FREE book

Regency London's wild child is about to meet her match…

If Lady Cecily Norris' parents are ashamed of her, they only have themselves to blame.

As a young girl, she was sent to live at a country estate along with other unwanted children of the *ton*. Her upbringing could only be described as unconventional and haphazard.

Cecily has now become a young woman both beautiful and wild at heart. Returning to London, she is determined to set her own rules for how she lives her life. As far as she is concerned, the *ton* and all its expectations for how a young unmarried woman should behave, can all go hang.

But she cannot fully escape her future, and her dismayed parents demand that she make a suitable and sensible marriage.

When Lord Thomas Rosemount trips over Cecily in a dark garden, he falls hard. His heart quickly follows.

In Thomas, Cecily encounters a man very different from those that she has lived with all her life. He is reliable, sensible, and dare she say a little boring?

But Thomas offers her something that she has never

known before. A home and a future with someone who loves her.

Thomas knows it will take more than pretty words and a kind heart to win Cecily's hand, and he will have to look deep inside himself to discover whether he is truly the man who can tame a Wild English Rose.

Join my VIP readers and receive your FREE copy of A Wild English Rose.

Prologue

April 1798
Cable Bay, Bermuda

Andrew McNeal tucked his loaded pistol into the back of his breeches. He reached for one of the lit torches, which hung from a bracket on the wall just inside the front door of his home.

"No lights," snapped his father.

His arm quickly dropped, and he fell in behind the rest of the small group of men as they headed outside. He knew better than to challenge his father's orders. At the ripe old age of thirteen, Andrew had already experienced first-hand the full fury of James McNeal's wrath. Being whipped in front of a ship full of pirates wasn't something he wished to ever endure again.

James McNeal led the group as they moved stealthily across the small clearing that had once been a well-tended garden, and into the cedar forest which abutted the yard of the now neglected property. The narrow path, which ran between the trees, led down to the beach.

Where are we going?

He desperately wished to ask that question, but the rule of silence was golden. His father was in the lead, followed by two of his most trusted men. Then came Andrew. Bringing up the rear was the towering form of Nevis, a former slave whom James had liberated from the island which gave him his name.

They were well clear of the house when a sharp whistle pierced the heavy night air. James held up his hand and the small party immediately came to a halt.

Nevis stepped up to stand alongside Andrew, placing a protective hand on his shoulder. The boy glanced up at the six-foot seven-inch man, but Nevis shook his head. He had no answer to Andrew's silent query. The purpose of tonight's expedition was strangely being kept a closely guarded secret.

Things must be dangerous if Nevis doesn't know what is happening. Father always takes him into his confidence.

Movement amongst the trees on the path ahead, had Andrew reaching under the back of his jacket and retrieving his pistol. He was about to cock the weapon when his father let out a sigh.

"About bloody time," said James.

"Kent to Bermuda is not quite the same as a leisurely stroll across Hyde Park," came the brisk reply.

The stranger in the dark was well-spoken, his accent similar to that of Andrew's father. The glow of a light appeared, and a smartly dressed gentleman came into view. He was accompanied by another man, who was also attired in respectable clothing. From their manner of dress, it was clear, they were not from this part of the world.

Andrew peered at them. The first man had facial features very similar to James. The same hook nose and slightly lopsided grin.

"Yes, well, your timing was always a little off, but I think you might have just made it with a minute or two to spare," replied James.

The two men greeted each other with the merest of hugs.

So, they do know one another.

As they drew apart, an almighty explosion boomed through the air. It was quickly followed by loud cries and the unmistakable sound of gunshots. Andrew whirled round to see flames leap high into the night sky.

He didn't need to ask Nevis what had just happened. It was obvious that James McNeal had finally made good on his threat to blow up Hezekiah Frith's ship. War had been declared in Cable Bay.

James chuckled. "I see you brought trouble with you."

The other man slowly shook his head. "You have always been more than capable of creating your own havoc, dear brother. Or are you going to pretend that you didn't have a hand in that piece of mischief?"

Andrew stifled a grin. Of course, his father was involved.

"It's my handiwork. That blackguard Frith has been overstepping again. Trading in slaves. I've told him more than once; I won't stand for it. Bermuda needs to have free men, not those bound in chains. Forcing him out of the privateering business is a clean sweep. A changing of the guard so as to speak."

"Speaking of changes. Is the boy ready?"

James's shoulders dropped. "You mean my son?"

"My heir."

With a tired sigh, James turned to Andrew. "Come here."

He did as he was told, stepping forward to stand near to his father. Andrew wisely remained just out of arm's reach. James's temper had a short fuse, and he never held back when a clip over the ear would add weight to his words.

"Andrew, this is your uncle William. Otherwise, known as his grace, the Duke of Monsale. He has come for you."

Andrew's mouth dropped open in surprise. "What? No."

His father had just shot him a warning glance, when a second explosion tore through the night.

Hezekiah Frith wouldn't have to bother about trying to repair his ship. There wasn't going to be anything left to salvage.

James beckoned Nevis to come forward. Nevis handed him a small chest, which James then passed onto his brother's servant. "This should cover the cost of raising the boy."

What is going on? He can't be sending me away.

"Father, I want to stay here with you. To fight. I am prepared to die if I have to," said Andrew.

The two McNeal brothers exchanged a knowing look. William's gaze then landed squarely on Andrew. "I take it you are as stubborn as your father. Good. You will need all that steely spine in the years to come. But tell me, are you also quick of mind boy?"

Andrew reached into his jacket pocket, then held his tightly fisted hand out in front. He slowly uncurled his fingers.

William McNeal glanced down at his nephew's hand and swore. "That's my bloody pocket watch. How the devil did you get hold of it?"

"You asked if I was quick. There is your answer."

There came a roar of gunfire and more loud shouting from up on the road above them. It clearly hadn't taken long for Frith's men to realize who had been behind the attack, and they were now bearing down on the McNeal house. Once they discovered no one was at home, they would more than likely head for the beach, following down the same path that Andrew and the rest of the small group had already taken. A violent mob, hell-bent on revenge would soon be bearing down upon them.

James grabbed a hold of Andrew, pulled him into a fierce hug, then shoved him into William's arms.

"Your grace, take the boy."

"But father, we need to fight!" Andrew pleaded.

His father closed his eyes and for the one and only time in his life, Andrew McNeal sensed James was suddenly unsure of himself.

But the moment passed all too quickly.

"If you die, the McNeal bloodline will fail. This is bigger than any of us," said James.

Hot tears sprang to Andrew's eyes. He hated them. Only women and small children cried. "But I don't want to go. Please."

His uncle slipped an arm around his shoulder. He pushed it away, refusing the offer of comfort.

As the noise of the mob grew louder, Nevis and the other men, raced back up the path in the direction of the road. James sucked in a deep breath. His face was a study of conflicted emotions. Of deep, regret-filled pain.

"I failed your mother. I will not fail you. Now go."

The man accompanying the duke, took a hold of Andrew's arm and pulled him away. Andrew glanced back over his shoulder, catching the words and sight of his father for what he feared would be the last time.

"Nihil necesse est cedere," said James.

He pulled his pistol out of his jacket pocket, cocked it, then gave Andrew one final nod. He took off after his men, back toward the house, and straight into the fight.

The Duke of Monsale, grabbed Andrew's other arm and between the two men they dragged the reluctant boy down the path, in the direction of the beach.

He fought them the whole way, desperate to go back to the house and help his father. "Cowards why are you running away from the fight?" he taunted them.

"Because your death would be an empty gesture. Your father is buying your life with his, now come on," snapped the duke, his voice heavy with emotion. The pain in his uncle's words shocked Andrew into silence.

Two hundred yards on and the narrow path ended at the edge of the forest. They stepped out onto the soft beach of Cable Bay. The light from the moon tinted the white and pink sand crystals a pale silver hue. Andrew had lived his entire life on the island, and yet, he still found the sight of the beach at night breathtaking.

But he didn't have time to linger and enjoy the view. His uncle tightened his grip on Andrew's shoulder, determinedly making his way toward a small rowboat which sat bobbing up and down on the water close to shore. Andrew's gaze quickly shifted from the boat, settling on the large, three-masted British naval frigate which was anchored some sixty or so yards, further out in the bay.

Andrew's steps faltered at the imposing sight. He wasn't used to being this close to one. His usual response to seeing a battleship such as this was to either hide in the forest, or if he was at sea, put every sail into the wind and make a run for it. The British navy were not known for showing pirates any sort of mercy.

This isn't right.

Violently wrenching himself free of the two men, he went for his pistol. He pointed it directly at his uncle.

"I don't need to go with you. It's only seven miles around the coast to the town of Hamilton, I've walked it plenty of times. I know good people who I can trust to keep me safely hidden until the danger has passed. Then I will return home to my father."

The duke sadly shook his head. "Andrew, you must know that there is every chance that your father is already dead. Which makes you now my heir. I sailed from England because James and I agreed that I would take you back to Monsale Castle with me. I shall raise you to become a gentleman. And when I eventually die, you will succeed me and become the Duke of Monsale."

Leave Bermuda? This is my home. Father cannot be dead.

Andrew's hold on the pistol wavered. "I don't want to go to England."

With his hands raised, William took a step forward. "My boy, there is nothing left for you here. Your future lies elsewhere."

"They are coming!" yelled the duke's aide.

A heavily armed mob crashed through the undergrowth a little further up the beach. Cries of "Kill them!" reached his ears.

Andrew had been in enough skirmishes and bloody battles in his few short years to know that these men meant business. They wouldn't even consider sparing a young lad. Especially not with his reputation.

"Move!" he cried and sprinted for the rowboat. Their only hope of salvation was the heavily armed frigate. Andrew waded out into the water and climbed on board the boat. His uncle's aide came next. The Duke of Monsale however remained on the beach. He was busy firing off both his pistols.

There was a riot of smoke and gunfire. The duke's guns brought several of the assailants down. Then more of the mob approached, screaming vile threats. Andrew couldn't make head nor tails of what was going on. His only concern was that his uncle wasn't making any attempt to reach the boat.

"Run!" Andrew bellowed.

The duke finally dropped his weapons and headed into the water. He was waist deep when a shot rang out, and he suddenly stopped. William glanced down at his chest, then lifted his head, and met Andrew's gaze. There was an odd expression of pained surprise on his face.

"Oh no. Your grace!" cried one of the crewmen.

The duke flinched as a second bullet hit him. He kept going, heading toward the rowboat; swimming as the water grew deeper. The crew raced to their oars, pulling hard, until they had drawn up alongside him.

It took the combined efforts of three men to haul him into the boat. As soon as he hit the bottom, all hands set to turn the vessel around and head out to sea.

While bullets fired from the shore continued to ping off the surface of the water, Andrew sat silent in the bow. He didn't want to look at his uncle. Death was something to which he was well accustomed.

The duke's man removed his jacket and placed it over the shivering William. It was night and the salty air of Bermuda was warm. A man could spend an hour or more in the water and still not feel a chill. But a wounded body would quickly lose heat as it went into shock.

"Andrew," whispered the duke.

He gritted his teeth and moved to sit beside his uncle. "Yes, your grace?"

"Our family has held Monsale Castle for over six hundred years. The line of dukes unbroken. Do you understand me?"

He nodded. "Father said the blood must not fail."

William tugged the jacket off his chest. Even in the pale moonlight, the dark patches of blood were clearly evident. There was little chance that William McNeal would survive the night, let alone make it back to England.

"Yes, it must not fail. That is the duty I now entrust you with, Andrew McNeal. Go back to England and make certain that our family survives. I'm sorry for the mess that the estate is in. Money has never been my strong suit."

His father was dead, and his uncle was fading fast. Soon he would be all alone in the world. Andrew couldn't remember a time when he felt such a sense of trepidation. Of fear.

"Please. Don't leave me. I will have no one," he begged.

The duke lifted his hand and pointed at the man who had accompanied him to the shore. "Adan will take care of you; he will see you safely to England. He knows much of the estate dealings. You can trust him."

England was so far away. A strange and mysterious land that Andrew knew little about. All he had ever heard from his father and other sailors was that England was a place from which men chose to flee. It was somewhere he hadn't ever planned to go.

He took a hold of William's hand. It was already cold. They sat quietly while the crew rowed out to the ship, Andrew's gaze flittered from the darkened shore to his fading uncle.

"What did my father mean when he said, 'Nihil necesse est cedere' to you?" he asked.

The duke gave a pained smile. "It's the McNeal family motto, part of our coat of arms. It means, nothing must be yielded. I thought you would already know that."

Andrew scowled at the words. His father had certainly been true to them, never once backing down. "Yes, I know the meaning. I just didn't understand why he had to say it to you when you parted."

The ship loomed closer. Ropes were tossed down to the rowboat. A stretcher was lowered over the side. Andrew moved out of the way while William was lashed to it. As he was lifted, the duke cried. "Halt!"

William held his hand out and with a sense of dread and foreboding Andrew stepped forward and took it once more. It was freezing. His uncle's body temperature was dropping rapidly.

William coughed up a mouthful of blood, the dark crimson staining his white cravat. "Your father meant that the most precious things had to be protected. And by that, he was referring to you, Andrew. You are the hope for our family's future. I came from England to collect you, so that the Duchy of Monsale would survive. It is now up to you to continue the bloodline."

His eyes rolled back in his head and his grip on Andrew's

hand fell away. A gurgling, rattling breath escaped William's lips.

"Heave away!" cried one of the crew.

The stretcher was hoisted over the side of the ship. Adan was hauled onboard by a separate rope. When it came back over the side, a hand tugged firmly on the sleeve of Andrew's jacket, "Take the rope, lad," said the sailor.

In a half daze Andrew grasped the line. He gave one last look back to the shore, then tugged on the rope signaling his readiness to come up. His feet lifted clear of the rowboat. As soon as he was level with the deck rail, he swung a leg over the side and dropped onto the floor of the frigate.

He hurried over to where his uncle lay sprawled on his back. His steps slowed as all those who had gathered around William, went down on bended knee. Hats were slipped off and heads quickly bowed.

No. Please lord. No.

In a matter of minutes, he had lost both his father and uncle. His world was forever changed. William's man Adan, rose and approached. He was followed by the ship's captain. They stopped several feet in front of Andrew and bowed low.

Don't say it.

"Your grace," they said in unison.

A shroud of anger quickly enveloped him. All sadness was swept away. There may well come a time for tears and grieving, but that was not this moment. Not this day.

The only thing which remained was the burning need for revenge. Andrew turned to the captain.

"Does this ship have any shot on board?" he asked.

Adan frowned but Andrew ignored him.

"It does, your grace. Your late uncle only borrowed *HMS Grafton* from the British navy for this expedition. They want it back as soon as it is returned to England. And while we may only have thirty men onboard who can man the cannons, we can still inflict serious damage if required," he replied.

The Monsale steward gasped. "Your grace, you can't seriously be considering aiming the ship's guns at the men on the beach, it would be a bloody slaughter."

Andrew raised himself up to his full height. He was still a good five inches shorter than the steward. "No, I am not going to attack the blackguards who just killed my uncle." He turned back to the captain. "You are to sail the Grafton around into the next cove. There you will find a ship ablaze. You are to sink it. When that is done, you are to turn the full force of the ship's weapons on the town. Raze every building to the ground. I want nothing left."

With a hasty bow, the captain hurried off, shouting orders left and right. Andrew turned his attention to Adan, fixing him with a hard glare.

"I don't know what sort of relationship you had with my late uncle but let me make things clear. That is the first and last time you ever dare to correct me. I am Andrew McNeal, the fifteenth Duke of Monsale, and my word is law."

There had been a changing of the guard. A new duke now stood in the place of the old one. Andrew was offering William's steward a clear choice. Accept his rule or resign his position. And while he very much wanted Adan's guidance, he was also determined to be the one who made the final decision.

The look of deep concern on Adan's face slowly faded to one of quiet acceptance. He would yield.

He bowed low. "Yes, your grace."

Chapter One

July 1817
A private party
London, England

"Happy birthday Monsale. Thirty-three today, you poor old thing," said Harry.

"Not old, and most definitely not poor," snorted Monsale.

Lady Naomi Steele stifled a laugh. Her brother Harry was always giving Monsale grief over the fact that he was older than the other members of the RR Coaching Company. But Monsale had the right of it when it came to wealth. Of all the rogues of the road, he was by far and away the richest.

And the only one still unwed.

The three of them were standing to one side of an overcrowded ballroom in an elegant mansion in Duke Street. And while Harry and Monsale were each nursing a large brandy, Naomi was doing her best to appear casually interested in watching a dull quadrille that was taking place. She wasn't in the mood for champagne.

Harry's wife Alice had cried off from tonight's festivities.

The exhausted new mother was at home getting some well-deserved sleep. A reluctant Naomi had been pestered into accompanying her brother this evening. Considering his former reputation as a society peacock, she thought it rather quaint that Harry had developed an aversion to attending social functions on his own.

The joy of being one half of a couple, I suppose.

Naomi turned and smiled at Monsale. "Yes, your grace, happy birthday, I wish you both health and happiness. And since your family is renowned for its longevity, I expect we shall have your company for many years to come."

Monsale raised an eyebrow. "Yes, well, only those family members who managed to avoid getting a stray bullet or a sword in their bellies were the ones graced with long lives. Fortunately, if my present run of luck holds, I should be able to look forward to making it to a ripe old age." He glanced down at his brandy glass, studying it for a moment. "It's the happiness bit I am not so certain of Lady Naomi— that appears to have eluded me."

Yes, well, a stone heart doesn't receive warmth, your grace.

Biting her tongue, Naomi turned her attention back to the dance. She would not be the one to make mention that a man could find happiness in the state of wedded bless.

I am willing to give you all my love for the rest of my life, Monsale. You simply have to ask.

Her generous offer did, however, come with some conditions. Monsale had to reciprocate her affections. To willingly offer up his own heart.

Naomi wouldn't ever enter into a loveless union. As far as she was concerned, spinsterhood was a far better option than being bound to a man who kept himself closed off from his wife's love.

Harry elbowed his friend in the ribs. "What you need to get yourself is a bride. A loving wife would bring you much joy. I can't believe I am saying this, but marriage has a great deal to offer a chap."

Lord Harry Steele had turned in his wicked party man card and become a dutiful husband and doting father. Naomi chanced a look at her brother, he was positively beaming. She had never seen him so happy. Love looked good on him.

If only she could say the same for herself. Unrequited love was a cruel burden at the best of times, at the worst— soul-destroying. Standing this close to the man who held her love so thoughtlessly in his hands had a familiar twinge of pain settling uncomfortably in her chest.

Why must loving someone hurt so much?

She had lost her heart to the tawny haired Monsale the first second she had laid eyes on him. He had been thirteen, she was a mere seven. And yet, there had been something about the poorly dressed Andrew McNeal which had captivated her, long before she knew what the word love truly meant.

Her father, the Duke of Redditch had taken the orphan boy-duke under his wing the moment he arrived in London. And with his careful guidance, he had helped Monsale to slowly pull the McNeal family finances back from the brink of bankruptcy.

When he finally reached his majority, Monsale had taken over the full management of his estate and through his own efforts had taken the dukedom's wealth to a whole new level. It was rumored that he was now one of the richest men in all of Britain. More affluent than even all the major banking families.

Yet no woman had managed to capture his heart. He remained, steadfastly, and in Naomi's opinion, stubbornly, a bachelor.

Why can't you see me? I am standing right here, ready to love you.

Naomi stirred from her musings as the music stopped,

and the quadrille came to an end. They applauded the dancers. Harry downed his glass of brandy and gave her a gentle nudge.

"Why aren't you twirling around the floor this evening, Naomi? I know you love to dance."

She gave a disinterested shrug. To her way of thinking dances like the quadrille, were boring. They lacked passion. Only a waltz would tempt her, and even then, it had to be with the right partner. The only man who held her interest was the same man who paid more attention to his drink than the entertainments which the party had on offer.

"I think I may have a touch of ennui. To be honest, dear brother, if you hadn't badgered me into accompanying you this evening, I would have likely stayed at home," she replied.

It was late July, and Naomi was just about at her wits end. The social season had seen her once more left on the shelf. Certain that they couldn't ever give her what her heart desired, she had refused marriage suits from two perfectly suitable noblemen.

At six and twenty, she was in grave danger of becoming a set-in-stone, spinster, an ape leader. No other duke's daughter of her generation remained unwed.

Her father and eldest brother had both assured her, she would never be compelled to marry. And while financial security was one thing Naomi didn't have to worry about, she still hadn't managed to overcome the problem of her aching need to be wanted. To have a man in her life who truly loved her.

I've half a mind to march up to Monsale and demand that he offers for me. I would make a wonderful birthday present. Something warm and willing for him to unwrap.

Harry leaned in and nudged her once more. "Come on Naomi, cheer up. Augustus and Evangeline are arriving from France later this week. You must be eagerly awaiting their wedding ball; I know Mama and Mrs. Jones are planning a party of special magnificence."

Naomi forced a tight smile to her lips. The last thing she needed was to attend a function where love was being celebrated. And while she was happy for Gus and eager to meet his bride, she found it a struggle to dampen down her own disappointment.

She quietly admired Gus Jones's grand gesture of love. Only a man who had lost his heart completely to a woman would give up his family, his country, and go to live with her in the ruins of an old château.

How romantic. Evangeline is a lucky girl. After all that Gus has been through, he deserves to be happy.

She was still lamenting her own lack of success with love when the orchestra struck up the opening strains of a waltz. Couples quickly gathered on the dance floor once more. Naomi's pink-slipper clad feet itched to dance.

It was time to take a chance.

Nothing ventured, nothing gained.

She stepped away from her brother and came to stand in front of his friend. A scowling Monsale peered down at her from his lofty height. "Lady Naomi."

It was a familiar game; one which they had played many times before. And all with the same outcome. She had always lost.

"Your grace. Would you be so kind as to indulge me with a turn or two around the dance floor?"

His brows furrowed in their all too familiar way. Anyone would think she was asking him to ride naked along Oxford Street such was the look of surprised distaste which appeared on his face.

"Dance?"

Naomi painted a smile on her lips. "Yes. That's when people move about together in time to music. It's really quite fun. I am sure you would enjoy it immensely if you would just try. I am quite accomplished when it comes to the waltz, so I promise we won't look foolish."

A duke's daughter reduced to begging. What has the world come to?

The frown on his face deepened. "I don't dance."

And there it was, yet another rejection. Why did she even bother?

Because you are a silly girl who still lives in hope that he will one day see the love which shines for him in your heart. And that he will decide he cannot live without you.

Her bitter frustration spurred her on. "Didn't you hear Harry as he extolled the virtues of wedded bliss not five minutes ago? You will never find a wife if you don't socialize with the fairer sex. And if you don't have a duchess, how is the McNeal family line to continue? You have a duty to make sure that the sixteenth Duke of Monsale is born, and the title passed on."

Naomi cursed the tears which threatened. How many more times would she make a fool of herself over this man?

Monsale glanced down at the glass of brandy in his hand. "I am in no haste. When I eventually feel that it is necessary for me to take on a wife, I shall do something about it. Until then…"

He couldn't even be bothered to give her a full answer. She wished nothing more than to punch Monsale. To knock some sense into him. To make him finally see that she was more than just Harry's little sister. That in her heart of hearts she knew they were destined for one another.

She blinked back the tears, determined not to show him, or anyone else her pain.

I should not have come this evening. When am I ever going to learn that he doesn't give a damn?

"If that's the case then you should be relieved to know that women are not lining up, to become your duchess. Excuse me, your grace, I have better places to be this evening. Happy birthday, Monsale. Enjoy the rest of your night."

She gave Harry a brief nod and headed straight for the door, taking what was left of her crumbling pride with her.

Monsale lifted his brandy to his lips and took a sip, all the while his gaze lingered on the retreating figure of Lady Naomi as she walked away. The duke's daughter was feisty, headstrong, and determined.

She was also thoroughly delicious.

The way her generous breasts filled out the top of her evening gown always made his heartbeat skip to a fast clip. And the fabulous sway of her hips and ass as she moved. Even in a foul mood, she had a certain allure about her.

If only you weren't so bloody tempting.

If she had been any other woman, he might have already given up the fight and married her. But Monsale was no fool. He knew full well that the man who did eventually marry Lady Naomi Steele was signing up for a life with a stubborn wife. She had made no secret of the fact that she would want a marriage of equals. To have a say in every one of her husband's major decisions.

The mere thought made him scoff. He had never been one for any sort of connection or relationship being based on an equal footing. In his business dealings people did as he instructed. Even the other members of the RR Coaching Company, his closest friends, and partners, yielded to his demands.

He'd had almost twenty years of no one daring to question, let alone countermand his commands. His loyal steward Adan had been the first and last to try it on that fateful day in Bermuda.

Monsale had long ago realized that acquaintances and

even friends could be easily manipulated, but the woman who made it plain that she wished to be his duchess was someone he knew he could not control. Lady Naomi had grown up a duke's daughter and was used to having people listen to her. In the Steele household, her opinions carried weight. She had power and influence. And that made her dangerous to a man like him.

She will challenge me. Expect to be my equal. I can't have that with anyone.

Monsale was utterly clueless when it came to being able to handle a woman such as Naomi. He knew enough from the marriages of his fellow rogues of the road that only a rash idiot would attempt to tame a wife. Naomi wouldn't ever stand for a man to tell her what to do.

She will bite the hand off the first person who tries to put a leash on her.

During his illicit career he had battled bloody pirates and taken on both the French and British navies, but when it came to dealing with headstrong women, Andrew McNeal, Duke of Monsale hadn't the foggiest notion as to what he should do.

And yet, you still want her.

His nights had long been filled with dreams of holding Naomi naked in his arms; of her long golden locks splayed out across the sheets of his bed. Of her soft sighs of sexual completion. Of knowing that he was the only man she loved. The only one who would ever possess both her heart and body.

What on earth am I going to do about her?

"You certainly have a knack when it comes to annoying the devil out of my sister," observed Harry.

Monsale lifted his glass to his lips, surprised to discover that it was, in fact, empty. When had he finished the last of his drink?

"I don't know why she insists on asking me to dance with her, she knows I never partake," he replied.

Harry gave a knowing hum. "One day some other chap will catch Naomi's eye. Might even sweep her off her feet and offer to marry her. The question you have to ask yourself, old chap, is, are you prepared to stand by and let that happen?"

And while Naomi was no longer a fresh debutante, she was still one of the major catches of the London *ton*. Her dowry and lineage were enough to have her firmly at the top of every noble matchmaking mother's list.

Harry's remark pulled Monsale up short. Doing his best to maintain his air of vague interest, he slowly turned and met his friend's gaze. "Is there someone else in your sister's line of sight? I mean an earl or a marquis she might be prepared to settle on?"

"Who knows. But eventually, she may tire of receiving a firm no from the lips of a certain duke and decide that hearing yes from someone else is enough on which to build a life. You have been warned."

Monsale was in sudden need of another stiff drink.

Would she? Could she really choose another over me?

And what if Naomi finally did give up on him and agreed to settle down with another chap? Some gormless lesser male whom she could dominate, and who would soon bore her to tears. It was a chilling prospect, one which would see all parties living out a miserable, bitter existence.

What if I do push her patience too far? If she gives up.

He was in no particular hurry to leap into the arms of wedded bliss, but Lord Harry's words gave Monsale reason for pause. There surely had to be a limit as to what Naomi would endure from him. She was a female, and her sights had to be set on finding a husband.

What would he do if he lost her? Naomi might well be stubborn, but she was the only woman Monsale could ever imagine waking up next to for the rest of his life.

This birthday evening had seen him presented with

several unexpected gifts. The prospect of Naomi choosing another over him, the most unwelcome of them.

Perhaps I should say yes to the occasional waltz.

But that would mean handing control to Naomi. Unable to reconcile his mind to such a foreign concept, Monsale set to grinding his teeth.

Could he willingly give up any sort of power to another person?

"Impossible," he muttered.

Chapter Two

Ten days later

One of the benefits of Monsale being extremely wealthy was that he was able to support less financially secure London celebrities such as the renowned cook and author Doctor William Kitchiner. His patronage ensured that he was in receipt of a, as rare as hen's teeth, invitation to the official launch of not only Kitchiner's cookbook *The Cook's Oracle* but the exclusive dinner which was to follow.

Monsale's excitement at the prospect of an evening of mouthwatering splendor dimmed somewhat as his carriage drew up close to number forty-three Warren Street, Camden. His driver couldn't make it to the front door as the Prince Regent's royal carriage was parked rather inconveniently in the middle of the road, effectively blocking the rest of the way.

The carriage, however, was the least of Monsale's concerns.

Damn. All the other guests will go hungry if Prinny gets his hands on the food.

But even the thought of missing out on the supper wasn't really the problem. A man was well entitled to be wide of girth, Monsale had no issue with that; it was gluttony that set his mood to dark. The Prince Regent had a well-deserved reputation for not only eating his hosts out of house and home but pressing them for money.

More than once, Monsale had been forced to dip his hand deep into his own pocket to stay in good with the future king. He could only hope that Doctor Kitchiner's food would keep the prince happy tonight.

Stay out of Prinny's way and all will be well.

This evening was meant to be a welcome respite from his complicated life. A moment where he could pretend to himself that he was someone else. Not the leader of the rogues of the road, nor even the Duke of Monsale. Just him. He hadn't been himself for many years, but deep inside, he hoped that the young boy who grew up digging his toes in the pink sands of Bermuda still existed.

No one knew that side of Monsale, not even his closest friends. Many people guessed that they had his measure, but none did.

His own reputation about London society was at times unclear. He had heard plenty of the spiteful rumors concerning his sudden rise to Duke of Monsale. Malicious tales that told the story of how thirteen-year-old Andrew McNeal had used a bloody blade to kill both his father and uncle on the same night in the wilds of Bermuda.

After committing the murders, he had seized both the title and his uncle's ship. Upon arriving in England, he had claimed the enormous Monsale wealth for himself.

Now that is pure fiction.

The fact that the dukedom was on the verge of ruin at the time, didn't ever seem to figure in the story. He had arrived in

London a wild, brutish orphan and that was more than enough for many *ton* folk to judge him unsuitable, and therefore an outsider.

He climbed down from his carriage and walked the rest of the way to Doctor Kitchiner's house.

Inside the cramped foyer of the modest home, Monsale picked up a copy of the new cookbook and flipped it open. It was good to be able to have something to show for all the money he had invested in the project.

His good humor quickly faded as he thumbed through the seemingly never-ending pages of rambling prefaces, advice to cooks, and guides to measures. He had got through more than a third of the book before he stopped. Disappointment sat heavy, his hopes for a light entertaining read effectively crushed.

Where are the damn recipes? This isn't what I gave him all that money to create.

He was tempted to put the book down, but persevered. When he finally spotted the contents page, Monsale sighed with relief.

Now this is more like it. Food to delight the reader.

His gaze roamed down the long list of recipes. Soups, sauces, fish, vegetables. The dishes seemed endless.

Monsale's stomach growled as he imagined how delicious Italian sauce with mushrooms would taste. He licked his lips.

I hope the book launch is quick, and we can get down to eating. I am famished.

"Ah, another lover of the art of food."

Monsale snapped the book shut and with a polite smile firmly nailed to his face, turned to greet the prince. He bowed low. "Your royal highness, it is both an honor and a pleasure to see you here this evening."

Prinny held out his hand and a perplexed Monsale took it. Unsure as to what he should do, he bowed once more. Normally, the prince barely gave a grunt in his direction. To be spoken to was most unusual. Requests for money normally came via the prince's private secretary.

Obviously, the rest of the invited guests are not nobility, and if that is the case then their purses won't be substantial enough for Prinny to be bothered wasting his time with them. Which means I am going to be stuck with him.

There went his evening.

"Did you see the recipe for wow-wow sauce? It looks fabulous," gushed the prince.

Monsale blinked. "I beg your pardon. Wow-wow sauce?"

Prinny laughed, as did the rest of his small retinue. "Yes, it's an invention of Doctor Kitchiner's." He pointed at the cookbook. "Recipe three hundred and twenty-eight. It has port, wine vinegar, mushrooms, and all manner of other things. Hence, its name. You keep saying wow, every time you find another ingredient."

"I see," replied Monsale.

He wasn't sure as to what was more unsettling. The oddly named recipe or that the Prince of Wales was being friendly toward him. Monsale's nerves were on edge.

What does he think he has over me? It must be something. There must be a reason for him being so nice to me. What could it be?

It couldn't possibly be anything about the movement of tax-free goods from France to England. Prinny had long been one of Augustus Jones's best customers. And while the Prince of Wales might have done some rash things in his time, Monsale was certain he wouldn't ever be so foolish as to mention that he had dealings with smugglers. And most certainly not in public. If it ever came to light that the future king had been stealing from the government coffers, a bloody revolution might well follow.

No. It had to be something else.

There were many things Monsale, and his friends had done over the years which might see them hauled before the courts. Or in his case, the House of Lords.

Deuce. Am I about to be arrested?

Monsale's senses kicked up to high alert. Was this the night when he might finally have to make use of his flee box, empty its precious contents, and make a run for the continent? Into a life of exile.

He swallowed deep, fighting to keep control. To force down his fear and show no emotion.

Don't panic. Monsale had a finely tuned network of well-paid sources working deep within the palace and the government. People who should be able to warn him if anyone was about to make a move and seek to have him arrested.

I bloody well hope so. They cost me a small fortune.

He got a hold of himself; this was not his first time dealing with an unknown threat. The occasion called for a light touch. Cheerful banter and the appearance of not having a care in the world.

But all the while his mind was racing. What had gone wrong?

Oh god, why did I venture out to a social event like this on my own?

Balls and major functions were far safer. He could hide in the numbers.

I really ought to take Lady Naomi up on her offer to dance. No one would be so gauche as to attempt to arrest me in the middle of a waltz.

A trickle of sweat slid down Monsale's back as the Prince of Wales stepped closer, a sly smile sat on his lips.

"So, Monsale, will we be seeing you at the royal gala next week? I have some wonderful entertainments planned for the guests. I just need to press-gang Doctor Kitchiner into helping with the food," said Prinny.

His laughter at his own feeble jest, had the hairs on the back of Monsale's neck standing to attention.

"I am sure he would be more than happy to serve his future king. If you like I could have a quiet word with him on your behalf— right this very minute. I live to serve your royal highness," replied Monsale.

It was common knowledge in London that Prinny loved to be constantly reminded that he was one step away from sitting on the throne. And while the regency made him king in all but name, he was still a prince in waiting.

When the prince smiled sweetly at him a second bead of sweat trickled down Monsale's back.

What the devil are you up to?

Whatever it was, there was every chance it was going to cause him trouble. Prinny wasn't one for showing grace or exchanging pleasantries, not unless there was a gain in it for him. There must be something that the prince wanted. But what?

What do I have that he feels it is worth his time to be nice to me?

Out of the corner of his eye, Monsale caught sight of an approaching footman bearing a tray of hot hors d'oeuvres. He made a strategic move sideways. Only a fool placed himself between Prinny and food. The servant had barely managed a respectful bow before the prince had liberated three of the morsels from the plate and stuffed them into his mouth.

Did you even take the time to look at them?

Monsale sensed an opportunity to make his escape. He bowed low and took a hurried step back, startled when another member of the royal entourage took a firm grip of his arm. The courtier leaned in. "Don't forget the gala next week, your grace. His royal highness expects you to attend."

"Of course, I would be both honored and delighted. I shall make certain that it is penned into my diary as soon as I return home."

He was far richer than the prince, and in many ways more powerful, but no one refused a direct request from the future king. Monsale of course had no intention of attending the gala. Rather, a mysterious illness would befall him on that particular night, and he would send his deepest regrets at being so suddenly indisposed. He made a mental note to ask Adan to pen the letter in advance.

His appetite gone, Monsale made his apologies and promptly left. Climbing back into his carriage, his mind was focused on the machinations of the Prince of Wales.

Whatever it is that I have, does he plan to ask nicely for it, or just take?

By the time Monsale returned home, he had a long and thoroughly unpleasant list compiled in his head. Things which he suspected Prinny would love to get his hands on, as well as the possible reasons as to why.

The hour was late, but he wasn't going to waste any time attempting to sleep. He marched up the main staircase of Monsale House, making a beeline for Adan's private sitting room. If the Monsale estate steward stuck to his usual evening routine, he would still be up.

He marched into the room. His temper simmered on the edge of boiling over into full-blown rage. "What the hell does Prinny have over me?"

The gray-haired Adan set his book aside and slowly rose from his chair by the fire.

"Your grace. What do you mean?"

Monsale raked his fingers through his sandy brown locks. "The fat royal brat was sweetly pleasant to me this evening. He even asked if I was coming to the royal gala at Carlton House."

The color drained out of Adan's face. The Prince Regent was never nice to people unless they could give him something of value, or worse, he could hold a particular thing over them. He was avaricious to a fault.

"I haven't heard a thing. But I will get onto it right away. Should I commence with your contingency plans?" said Adan.

Monsale closed his eyes, racking his brains as to what could possibly make the prince speak to him in such a charming manner. He didn't want to panic, but it would be reckless for him to turn a blind eye to this sudden development.

"Have the yacht brought down the coast closer to Dover. In the morning, start working our sources for information. Someone has to know what he is up to, Prinny is not known for being subtle, especially if it means he can lord it over one of us. Me in particular."

In the morning, Monsale would send word to Harry, Stephen, and George, informing them of this evening's events. His note would also include directions for the rest of the England-based rogues of the road to immediately set to work on uncovering any sort of plans the prince may have with regard to the Duke of Monsale. If the English establishment were finally going to make a move on him, he wasn't going to go down without a fight.

His friends had to know that they were also likely in danger. They may well have given up their criminal ways, but if the hammer was about to fall heavy on him, they would surely be next.

Adan made his way to the door, then stopped.

"To my way of thinking, Spain is currently the best option for a safe haven. The Spanish have enough going on in their country without wishing to deal with the trifling matter of an English duke on the run. I will have the travel trunks made ready for us."

Monsale had friends in the north of Spain who would gladly give him sanctuary. Powerful men with connections in high places.

And while the choice to flee England would be hard enough for him, he wasn't prepared to impose a life of exile on his loyal steward. Adan deserved to make his own choices.

"Keep our trunks separate. If they do decide to make a move, I want you to undertake a fast run to Monsale Castle and retrieve the chest. Where you go after that, will be your decision, not mine."

No one need to make mention of the pirate's treasure that Monsale had hidden in the family crypt at Monsale Castle. His steward was the only other person who knew that while the young Duke of Monsale had arrived in England dressed in tattered clothing, he had secretly brought with him the small chest which Nevis had handed over that fateful night in Bermuda. A chest filled with gold Spanish doubloons.

The contents of the chest were more than enough to allow the loyal Adan the freedom to decide whether he would follow his master into exile or start a new life on his own terms.

The steward reached for the door handle, then turned back to Monsale. "I swore a lifelong oath to serve the McNeal family and that is what I intend to do. I've yet to see your grace walk away from a fight, and I don't expect I ever will. And while there is no shame in making plans, wherever you go—so do I."

The pirate within him stirred and Monsale grinned. "Whatever it is that the prince thinks he has over me, he has no idea of what I am capable of doing."

If the future king of England thought the Duke of Monsale was going to be an easy target, he was in for one hell of a shock.

He doubted the residents of Tucker's Town, Bermuda would ever forget the night that the guns of one of His Majesties frigates, were let loose upon the rough, shanty town, reducing it to rubble.

But since that day, when a young Monsale had stood on the deck watching the fires of his revenge light up the night sky, he had learned to steady his hand. To find darker, more secretive ways to bring his enemies down.

Committing treason against the British crown was not

something that even a duke undertook without a great deal of concern for its bloody repercussions.

"Please let it be something else, something which I can control," he muttered.

Lady Naomi Steele's words slipped back into his mind

You have a duty to make sure that the sixteenth Duke of Monsale is born and the title continues.

If it came down to a fight against the powers that be, he might well have to bend, to stop from breaking. It went against everything he had ever done, but his loyalty to the McNeal family was all that truly mattered. The line must be preserved.

Chapter Three

It took the better part of two days for the combined resources of the RR Coaching Company and his own select network of spies for Monsale to finally get an answer to the pressing problem of the Prince of Wales.

Late in the afternoon a knock came at the door of his study. Adan stepped into the room. "Lord Harry Steele, Sir Stephen Moore, and the Honorable George Hawkins," he announced.

Monsale rose from his desk as the remaining London-based members of the rogues of the road filed into the room. Adan closed the door behind him and locked it.

"Your grace. The moment I received word from my connection at Carlton House, I immediately sent for these gentlemen to attend you," he announced.

This doesn't look good. I might be sailing for Spain tonight.

The news must be dire for his steward to have gone ahead and arranged this meeting without his prior notice.

I could always sail on to Rome. I've always wanted to see the Vatican and the ancient Roman ruins. The Colosseum is meant to be quite the sight.

If he was going to have to flee England, he had better

settle on an immediate destination. Once safe, he could then take his time to decide where he might like to begin a new life. He had managed to do that once before; there was no reason why he couldn't do it again.

Yes, but you left behind little more than memories when you gave up Bermuda.

He'd had almost twenty years to put down roots in the land of his forefathers. Time in which he had restored the family fortunes and rebuilt much of Monsale Castle. Leaving his ancestral home would cause him soul deep pain.

Not to mention the woman who regularly filled his dreams.

While his friends all settled themselves on chairs and sofas, Monsale took up a spot perched on the end of his desk. He twiddled nervously with the gold signet ring on his left hand. If his friends did happen to notice his uncharacteristic discomfort, they wisely said nothing. It was a small blessing, and he was grateful for it.

Monsale leveled his steward with a sharp glare. "Don't keep me in suspense any longer. Whatever it is, just put me out of my bloody misery. Then I can start to formulate a plan," he snapped.

Adan shot him a disapproving look. The old man had served the previous duke for many years; William McNeal had not been one for foul oaths or wicked living. Then again, Monsale didn't have much of an opinion of his late uncle. Considering the terrible condition of the Monsale estate when he had come into his inheritance, it was clear the late duke hadn't been one for much of anything. He hadn't even managed to secure the hand and dowry of a wife.

The steward cleared his throat and addressed the gathering. "Your grace, my lords, gentlemen. Let me take you on a journey into the dim and distant past. All the way back to the month of August in the year of our lord, twelve hundred and seventeen. Six hundred years ago."

Sir Stephen groaned. "This is going to take some time, isn't it? I knew I should have eaten more at breakfast. Bridget is always telling young Toby, that the first meal of the day is the most important. I should do as my little brother does and heed her advice."

Monsale softly chuckled. Trust Stephen to find a way to cut through the tension in the room. "I promise to feed you all, before I make a run for the continent," he replied.

"For those of you who don't know your history, the deeply unpopular King John had sat on the English throne until late the previous year. During the latter part of his reign the barons and other nobles revolted," continued Adan.

Monsale's ears pricked up. *I know this part.*

"And the McNeal family sided with the barons," said Monsale.

His father might well have neglected him, but James had gone to great pains to ensure that his son received as best an education as could be provided on the island. He was always on the lookout for good tutors; and was not above kidnapping the odd one if he felt they had the skills to teach the young Andrew something of value.

"After King John died and Henry came to the throne, the Duke of Monsale shifted the family allegiances to him."

Adan screwed up his face. "Yes, but not until after the Battle of Sandwich in August of twelve seventeen. Before that time, your forebear was still on the side of the French who were seeking to take the English crown. After the French lost the battle, the McNeal's changed sides. But the duke was made to swear a public oath of fealty to King Henry."

Monsale quickly having lost interest, gave a half shrug. What did an ancient skirmish some six hundred years ago have to do with him? Or his current issues with the Prince of Wales.

Adan took a deep breath. "From what I have discovered that oath must be sworn again every hundred years. If it is not, then all the Monsale titles and lands will be declared forfeit and handed over to the crown. Before the end of August, your grace, must kneel before the prince and reaffirm your family loyalty."

"Bloody hell," muttered Harry.

"You had better get your oath swearing up to scratch," said George. Stephen's stomach rumbled its agreement.

Monsale gave a small glance at his friends, then refocused on Adan. From the dour expression on the man's face, there was obviously more to come.

"What else?"

"You and your wife must swear the oath."

"I don't have a wife."

Adan nodded. "And therein lies the problem. You have until the twenty-fourth of August to find a bride. Unless you and your wife kneel before the Prince of Wales on that day, reaffirm the McNeal family loyalty to the crown, you will lose it all."

Monsale let out a huff as he pushed off from the desk. Little wonder the prince was being so solicitous toward him. The two-faced regent was just biding his time before he came and gleefully demanded that Monsale hand over the keys to his life.

But how is it that I had never known about this? I've not heard a soul mention anything about an oath.

"So, what you are telling me is that Prinny has somehow managed to discover this long-forgotten snippet of history and plans to use it to further his own interests?" replied Monsale.

He could just imagine the prince wringing his hands with unrestrained glee at the prospect of getting hold of the wealth of the Dukes of Monsale. It would certainly solve a lot of his well-known financial problems.

"Yes, apparently he has a whole team of people searching back through historical records looking for ways and means for him to seize ancient noble wealth. You are not the only one he has in his gun sights."

Harry rose slowly from his seat on the sofa and crossed the floor. The worried look on his friend's face did nothing to ease Monsale's concerns. It was a rare thing to see Lord Harry Steele in anything besides a jovial mood.

He stopped a foot or so away. When George did the exact same thing and came to stand alongside Harry, Monsale held his breath.

I'm the one for staring people down. For making uncomfortable offers. Not them.

"Go on say it."

"Monsale. You have exactly two weeks before you and your wife have to kneel before the Prince of Wales and swear your allegiance to the crown," said George.

Harry nodded. "Or to put it more succinctly. Woo. Wife. Wedding. Wales."

He flinched at the remark. Marriage had suddenly gone from a long way down on his list of priorities all the way to the top.

The London season had recently ended. This year's pick of the debutantes and diamonds of the first water had already been snapped up. Eligible, obedient young women coming from the right sort of blue bloodlines would be thin on the ground.

But you don't want a biddable wife.

He hadn't put a lot of thought into the sort of woman who make a good life partner, but he knew what he didn't want. Sweet society girls had never stirred his loins. Which left one clear candidate.

How do I get her to marry me without handing her my manhood on a platter?

He would gladly give Prinny his last farthing before he would beg the only woman who had ever captured his interest to marry him. There had to be another way. For her to offer herself up gladly— nay, eagerly to be his wife.

"There is of course one lady who would be perfect for the role," said George.

Monsale held up his hand. "Please don't offer any suggestions. Thank you, gentlemen. I can as always rely on my friends for honest advice. But I think I need to engage the services of someone with a different set of skills in order to forge a safe path through the dark wood ahead."

Monsale turned to his steward. "Have the town carriage made ready. I need to go out."

He was off to see the only female in all of England who could understand the bind he was in; the only woman who would make certain of his plan's success.

Lady Kitty Steele, the Duchess of Redditch. Naomi's mother.

Chapter Four

"Well, you must give him his dues, the Prince of Wales is simply looking to capitalize on the situation. The first Duke of Monsale is the one who is really to blame. And it's not Prinny's fault if you were not aware of the oath, or that its sixth hundredth anniversary is shortly to be upon us. By getting his hands on your money, he would be able to pay off most of his creditors. That would put him back in a position of power, especially with the government."

Cup of tea in one hand, and notebook in the other; seated on the edge of the cushion of one of Lady Steele's overstuffed floral sofas, Monsale could only nod his reply.

Kitty, of course, was right. Though he couldn't find it in his heart to blame his long dead ancestor for having picked the wrong side in a fight for the English crown. He was quietly reserving his wrath for whomever it was in the royal court who had managed to unearth the long forgotten ancient law and then brought it to the prince's attention.

I would love to get my hands on the observant little toe-rag who discovered this bloody oath. He could do with a good throttling.

The question of whom and how had sat in the forefront of his mind since leaving his home in Mount Street a short time earlier. It was a brief stroll to Redditch House in nearby Grosvenor Street, but Kitty had a particular liking for visitors to arrive properly. And that meant graciously in a carriage.

"I'm holding back on giving my opinion of Prinny. Firstly, to save your delicate ears, but mostly, so I can find a way to get back at him when this whole marriage farce is over," replied Monsale.

The duchess harrumphed. "For a start my ears have had plenty of practice listening to my husband. I doubt that there exists a foul word which has not reached me over the years. But if you are serious about securing a suitable wife for yourself, I would caution you not to go speaking the words marriage and farce all in the same breath. Prospective brides and their families are likely to take umbrage at hearing such a thing."

Suitably chastened, Monsale set his cup and saucer down on a nearby table. He opened the notebook and retrieved a pencil from his jacket pocket. "My apologies Kitty. As you can no doubt understand, this has all come as a bit of a shock. Here was I worrying about the precious roses which are due to arrive from Morocco this week and the next thing I know, I have two weeks in which to save my family title and lands."

The duchess sat forward on her sofa. There was an unmistakable glint in her eye. Monsale steeled himself for the next exchange.

"So why are you here, Andrew?"

He may well be a duke, but to Lady Kitty Steele, he would always be the young, orphaned Andrew McNeal.

Monsale turned the pages of the notebook, until he found a blank sheet. "I need names. A list of potential brides. I am hoping, no I am praying, that you will be able to help me."

Kitty's eyes grew wide. He could just imagine what was going through her mind this very moment. Panicked male throws himself at the feet of one of the most senior matrons of the *ton* and pleads for her assistance in finding a bride. If it had been anyone other than Harry's mother, she would have likely laughed at him.

But the duchess had been one of the first people to take Monsale under her wing when he arrived in London. She had introduced him to her son Harry, and the rest had been history. Kitty was always someone he could rely upon for honest, sensible advice.

She pointed at the notebook. "How many girls do you want on the list? With the season over, many people have already left London to summer at their country estates. But I could write privately to several good families who I know have eligible daughters. Girls who for various reasons didn't find a suitable husband this year. I could seek their level of interest, and if things looked favorable, invite the young ladies and their mothers to return to town," she offered.

He shook his head. Letters up and down the country would take days, if not weeks. Then there was all the time that travel would involve. A day lost here or there, and he might well find himself in the position of having to make a hurried proposal to an entirely unsuitable female, based purely on the fact of her being in London at the right moment.

Begging was not part of his plans. It simply wasn't going to happen. He was, after all a prized catch. He had a title, lands, and more than a few pennies in the bank.

Not to mention the money, he had hidden away in a number of secret bank accounts, as well as the cache of jewels he kept in the safe beneath the stables of the RR Coaching Company in Gracechurch Street. Monsale was in anyone's language filthy rich.

I just need a short list. As long as Naomi is on it, I will be satisfied. Then we can have a week of pretending I am searching for a bride before she and I announce our betrothal.

He had it all sorted and settled in his mind. All Kitty really had to do was to make sure her daughter saw things as clearly as he did. And while their courtship might not be the sweet one, she likely imagined in her private dreams, in the end she was getting what she had always wanted. Him.

I fancy your daughter. I know she has a thing for me. Give it a few weeks of sated bliss during our honeymoon, and I am certain she will get over any of her issues as to how we got to the altar. She might even decide she doesn't need an equal partnership after all.

He wouldn't have to yield up his heart or his power.

Lady Naomi McNeal, Duchess of Monsale. Problem solved.

But he still intended to make Naomi work for what she wanted. To his way of thinking it would give her a sense of accomplishment at the end. It wouldn't do to simply ask for her hand in marriage, Naomi had to feel that she had achieved victory. And the only way he could see that happening was if she had some competition.

Besides, a little prick of jealousy will help to make things more interesting. Give the whole courting experience some spark. I am certain that Naomi will understand.

"Thank you, Kitty, but we don't have time for back and forth. Just select the girls who are in town at present. That way I can get a good idea of their temperament fairly quickly and rule out those ladies who will not suit. Do you have anyone in mind?"

The duchess tapped her finger contemplatively against her lips. Monsale looked away. Kitty had the same complexion as her daughter, it wouldn't do for him to go staring at his friend's mother while his mind was focused on Naomi. On what finally getting his hands on her naked, luscious body would be like.

"I can think of one or two who might do at a pinch. And what about you, was there any young lady you would like me to put on the list?" she replied.

Her gaze locked firmly with his. The Duchess of Redditch was a woman not to be underestimated. Monsale attempted to hold his ground but failed. Few people could go up against him and not wilt, unfortunately Kitty was one of those rare people who he couldn't rattle.

He managed as best a nonchalant shrug as he could.

Kitty blinked slowly. "No one?"

"Well, if there is any chance of…"

His nerve faltered. If he asked Kitty to put Naomi's name on the list, it would likely create expectations on both the part of mother and daughter. Kitty no doubt would think Naomi was a perfect candidate for the role of his duchess, whereas Naomi would be waiting for him to fall at her feet.

Blast. Damned if I do and damned if I don't.

No. He wouldn't make mention of Naomi. Kitty would have to talk to her daughter and make certain that sense prevailed. There was not a noble mother in all of England who would be foolish enough to let the opportunity for their daughter to marry into one of the oldest titles in the country slip through her fingers.

Calm down. Naomi wants you, so she will make sure to put her name on the list. You are just going through the motions. Give her some competition and she will surely rise to the occasion. She will say yes.

"Sorry, was there a name you wished me to include?" replied Kitty.

"No, I will leave that in your capable hands. I am sure you will come up with three or so young ladies who will fit the bill."

He didn't like the sly grin which now sat on the duchess's face, but as long as it meant she was going to put Naomi's name at the top of the list, Monsale was more than content to pretend he hadn't noticed that look.

He got to his feet and gave Kitty a low bow. "Thank you so much for seeing me at such short notice, your grace. I won't take up any more of your day."

She rose from the sofa and offered him a brief hug. "I shall have the list ready for you by the morning. I expect you will want to get started on the selection process as soon as possible."

"Yes. Time is not something I have in abundance. I'm seeing my solicitor this afternoon to begin the process of marriage settlements. I spoke to Harry earlier, and he made me realize that there is a lot more involved in planning a wedding apart from standing in front of a minister."

He headed for the door and the next of his meetings. If things went according to plan, Lady Naomi Steele's name would be the one penned in those contracts.

Don't let me down Kitty.

Naomi waited by the window in the downstairs sitting room, quickly slipping behind a curtain as Monsale stepped out the front door of her family home. The last thing she needed was for him to catch her spying.

The moment his carriage drew away and into the traffic of the busy street, she lifted her skirts and scurried upstairs. With a hurried knock, she entered Kitty's drawing room. Her mother turned from the window and gave her a look, one which said she had been expecting Naomi.

Reading her mother's expression, she dropped her intended offhand inquiry, and got straight to the point. She had already surreptitiously checked with the servants that Monsale hadn't called in to Redditch House, in order to see her father. He had been to visit Kitty.

"Why did Monsale come to see you, Mama?"

"Have a seat, you and I have urgent, important matters to discuss," replied Kitty.

Her interest piqued; Naomi made herself comfortable on one of her mother's soft sofas. The cushion was warm, as if someone had recently been sitting on it. The thought that it may well have been Monsale, made her heart skip a beat.

Spying an untouched piece of cake sitting on the table next to her, she quickly snatched up the plate.

Orange tea cake, perfect.

Kitty shook her head as Naomi stuffed a generous piece into her mouth. "That was Monsale's, he didn't want it. I sometimes forget that he isn't one for tea and cake. Having spent his younger years in foreign climes, his tastes are not that of your typical Englishman. When I know that he is coming to see your father, I usually make sure that cook has baked some cornbread for him."

Naomi finished her mouthful, then set the plate to one side. She needed answers more than food.

"So why the sudden visit with you today?" she asked.

Lady Steele took a seat next to her daughter. It was only then that Naomi noticed the piece of paper in her mother's hand. On it were written two names.

"Monsale has an urgent and rather pressing need to find himself a wife. In less than two weeks he has to be married and then kneel in front of the Prince of Wales and swear an oath of allegiance. Apparently one of his forebears, some six hundred years ago, was on the wrong side of a battle. This caused grave offense to the crown. If Monsale doesn't meet the conditions of the ancient peace agreement, he forfeits his title and lands. And since he has such a short timeframe, Andrew came to me and asked that I put together a list of potential brides."

Naomi froze. Stunned at her mother's words.

Monsale has to marry. Within the next few weeks. He finally needs a wife.

She slowly shook her head, trying to fathom the reason as to why Monsale would need a list of potential brides. "I'm sorry. Did you say he wants you to make a list?"

"Yes. He figured I know enough people in London to have

a good idea as to which families have eligible and suitable daughters. Two girls immediately came to mind. I was thinking that perhaps you might like to be the third."

For a moment Naomi wasn't certain what she should say. Several uncouth words sat readily on the end of her tongue, but she held them back.

The only name that should be on that piece of paper is mine. There shouldn't be a list.

If there was any justice in the world, Monsale would have already been to see her father. The Duke of Redditch would have granted his provisional blessing, then demanded that his daughter be given a proper courtship.

Papa would have made it clear that Monsale has to dance with me. That I should be wooed.

Tears pricked at her eyes. Disappointment and embarrassment mixed with a shot of anger made for a bitter tasting cocktail.

She couldn't believe that Monsale expected her to compete with other women for the position of his duchess. It might well be called the marriage market, but Naomi would be damned if she was going to stand alongside all the other available livestock and await Monsale's inspection.

The nerve of that man. Here he was in desperate need of a wife, yet he still felt it necessary to put her through the humiliation of having her name on a list of candidates.

Like hell. I am not a prized filly for men to look in the mouth and check my teeth.

Her decision was made. "As you know full well Mama, I have never been one for purely making up the numbers. If Monsale wants a third name, you had better find someone else."

She had half a mind to snatch the paper from out of her mother's hand and toss it into the fire. That's how little she thought of the Duke of Monsale's absurd plans for selecting a wife.

"But Naomi my dear. I thought you would be delighted to be considered for the position of Monsale's duchess. You haven't exactly made a secret of the fact that you have a soft spot for him," replied Kitty.

Naomi got to her feet. She was barely holding back a torrent of angry tears.

"What I feel for him is obviously not a factor in his thinking. If it was, he wouldn't be asking you to make a list. He would be in Papa's study right this very minute asking for my hand."

The nerve. The cheek. That bloody obstinate man.

She was furious, mortified, but worst of all, she was in shocked pain. In asking Kitty to create the list, Monsale had stuck a knife in Naomi's heart. Her private hopes that she was the only one for him had shattered, along with her dreams. If he truly cared for her, she would have been the first and last woman he had in mind to marry.

Her years of longing for him, and loving him from afar, now revealed themselves to be nothing more than empty shells of hope. It was almost too much to bear.

Straightening her back, Naomi gathered what was left of her pride. She might well be bruised, but she was not defeated. Her hopes to become Monsale's duchess lay in tatters, but she was a duke's daughter, and her unbreakable sense of self-worth would see her through this heartache.

I've clearly been blind with my love for him all this time. Monsale views me as being no different from any other woman. He will never gift me his heart.

"Mama, please don't put my name on the list. I would rather suffer now, than make the mistake of marrying a man who doesn't love me. I am sure Monsale will find a young woman willing to become his duchess, one who will understand and accept the kind of marriage he intends to offer."

One without love.

"But while I am not prepared to be on the list, I am more

than willing to help with the selection process. I shall put together a dossier on each of the ladies you present to Monsale. Giving him a clear idea of their backgrounds, likes and dislikes is the least I can do."

Leaving her mother, Naomi headed upstairs to her bedroom. She made it most of the way before the tears finally won out.

Chapter Five

T*hirteen days to go.*

The letter from the Duchess of Redditch arrived at Monsale House early the following morning. An eager Monsale broke open the seal on the paper and unfolded it. He took one look at the names and swore. Naomi's name wasn't on the list.

"Bloody stubborn woman. All you had to do was offer up your name. After I had briefly met and then ruled out the other ladies, you would have been the last one standing. Then we could have started planning the wedding," he muttered.

Deuce. I think I might have misjudged this whole list thing. Naomi has clearly taken this the wrong way, and not put her name up.

He stared at Kitty's note for a time, in two minds as to what he should do next. The obvious would be to march straight over to Redditch House and ask Naomi to marry him. To confess that, he had made a mistake and that she was the only woman he had ever considered as being the right one.

And she will make me pay for it every day for the next fifty years.

What was he to do? The other and possibly riskier option was to call her bluff. Go ahead with the list and see how long it took until Naomi finally came to heel. She might have her pride, but he was certain that she wanted to be his wife.

Yes. That's what I will do. Make her be the one who does the groveling.

He could just picture how that would look. She would be in tears, pleading her case. Begging him to marry her. Confessing her love. Giving him what he wanted.

Offering up those sweet rosy lips for my hungry kisses.

That was a much more attractive solution.

Monsale was a man who had lived his entire life managing threats and solving problems. There were few perils he hadn't already faced and conquered. Getting Lady Naomi Steele in front of a priest shouldn't be too difficult. And the wedding vows did include her having to promise to obey.

She just has to be made to see sense.

A sly grin crept across his lips. He still had one perfect weapon at his disposal.

Jealousy. He intended to fully exploit it.

Chapter Six

T*welve Days to go.*
The hunt for a bride begins

Naomi smoothed the skirts of her ice blue silk gown and gave a slow glance around the ballroom. It might be August and the London social season well over, but there were still enough people in London ready to attend a hastily arranged ball or party.

Normally, the Steele family would be in the throes of closing up their London house and preparing to head north to the family estate, where they would spend most of the rest of the summer. But not this year. Kitty, having put the list together for Monsale had announced that they were going to remain in town until he had selected a bride. The next trip the duke and duchess would be taking would be to Monsale Castle in Kent for Andrew McNeal's wedding.

Naomi had voiced the feeblest of protests about this arrangement, before promptly making an appointment with her modiste. Assisting Monsale in his search for a wife would require the purchase of new gowns. There was comfort to be had in shopping.

The Steele family had arrived early at the function this evening, Kitty was keen to make sure everything was ready for Monsale when he met with the first lady on the bridal list. Naomi didn't know the owners of the mansion, and she didn't particularly care to circulate and socialize. She was here on a mission.

As soon as she entered the gathering, she looked for the nearest servant bearing a tray of drinks and made a beeline for them. Two quickly downed glasses of champagne took the edge off her nerves.

She was watching the other guests mingle, and toying with the idea of whether it was wise to go and find a third glass of champagne, when her nose caught a familiar scent. The hint of a man's cologne that she knew only too well.

He is here.

"Good evening, Lady Naomi."

She composed herself, then turned to face him. The sight which met her eyes, had Naomi swallowing deep.

Monsale was always well turned out for these sorts of events, but the sharp cut of his evening jacket and the tight fit of his black trousers informed her that he too had purchased a new wardrobe for the occasion. His hair was neatly cut and there wasn't a hint of his usual sexy, scruffy facial hair.

He is taking this bride choosing business far too seriously.

"Your grace. You look well," she said, in a voice as calm as she could make it.

Don't let him see you are rattled.

Her capacity for small talk was somewhat limited by her secret disappointment at seeing him so elegantly attired. He was obviously keen to make a good impression on the families of the ladies Kitty had selected.

Not for the first time, did Naomi wonder if refusing to be on the list had been a major misstep on her part.

But in the aftermath of her tears, she had come up with a different strategy. She would take him on at his own game. Show Monsale just what he was missing. What marriage to another woman would lack.

Hold your hand firm and steady on the tiller. This ship will come safely to harbor.

He bowed low to her. When he lifted his head, their gazes met. "You look stunning in that blue gown. Is it new?"

She smiled sweetly at him. "This old thing? I think it is last year's style. No point in wasting new clothes when I am just here as a bystander. Or should I say, to act as your assistant."

Monsale narrowed his eyes. "What do mean assistant?"

Time to put the plan into action.

"Didn't Mama tell you? I am here to give you all the pertinent details about the families and the girls on your list."

Which really means I am going to give you all the juicy gossip about them so that you can strike them off that bloody list and finally realize that you are a clod.

Only when he was ready to admit his mistake, confess that he wanted her with his heart and soul, would she budge an inch. In the meantime, there was sport to be had. Punishment to be inflicted.

"Kitty, I mean Lady Steele, didn't make mention of you playing a role. Don't feel obliged," he stammered.

It took all her strength not to clap her hands with glee. Watching the mighty Monsale squirm was particularly enjoyable.

"It is my pleasure. I only wish to see you happily settled with a good woman. And your lands and titles kept intact."

Monsale met her gaze for a long moment. The sly grin which slowly crept across his lips, all but shouted *challenge accepted.*

"Well, shall we begin? The first lady on your list is Miss Constance Harforde. Her family, while not in possession of a title can trace their lineage all the way back to William the

Conqueror. They are very old money. And well aware of their status in society."

He screwed up his face. Over the years, Monsale had made no secret of his dislike of snobs. There had been people, who unwisely looked down their noses at him. According to her brother Harry, Monsale had made certain that every single one of them was made to pay dearly for their arrogance.

"What can you tell me about Constance?" he replied.

"Well, they don't call her constantly delightful Constance for nothing. She has been raised on a steady diet of self-importance. The two of you should suit."

Naomi casually glanced at the silver bangle on her wrist, all the while silently congratulating herself for having made such a smart quip.

From what she could recall, Constance was spoiled and with a reputation for running to her well-heeled papa whenever things didn't go exactly according to her dictate.

With any luck Miss Harforde, would be off Monsale's list by the end of the night.

She pointed out a middle-aged couple who were slowly making their way across the floor. They were headed directly toward Monsale. Behind them trailed a tall, thin young woman, dressed in a high-necked white gown.

"Well here comes your first potential bride. Though you may need to get past her father before you are permitted to actually speak to her. I wish you a good evening, your grace."

After a quick curtsy, Naomi went to walk away. Monsale hurried after her, taking a hold of her arm.

"Naomi, wait. I want to ask you something. Why isn't your name on the list?"

She gave a disinterested wave of her hand. "That's not a question you should be posing to me, your grace. I would say that the only person who can truly answer that particular conundrum, is your good self. Whatever your reasons for creating that list, they must be sound. Because otherwise, only a simpering buffoon would throw away the best chance he had."

Monsale muttered something under his breath and let go of her arm. He was still grumbling as Naomi walked away. She wasn't going to spare him another moment of her precious time.

While she didn't exactly consider herself to be a bird in the hand, if he felt the need to go chasing after wildlife in the bushes, as far as she was concerned Monsale was more than welcome. Hopefully, a few nights of dealing with other women would cure him of his stubborn stupidity.

But what if the list does work if he can stand one of them enough to offer her marriage. What then?

That was the question Naomi didn't wish to consider. It was a dangerous game she was playing, the stakes high. If she failed, her heart would be crushed.

If he chooses another, then he never really loved me.

If that was the case, then she was better off without him. Time would eventually heal her wounds. And she wouldn't be left with regrets.

But if she did manage to succeed in having him declare his heart, a lifetime of love with Monsale would be her reward. She was determined not to settle for anything less.

"Monsale."

The one-word usage of his name, not 'your grace' should have been the first sign that Mister Harforde considered himself above a mere duke. Monsale gritted his teeth and turned to greet Constance's father. He was tempted to chase after Naomi and continue their discussion, but since Kitty had gone to such pains in order to arrange this introduction, he felt obliged to stay.

"Mister Harforde is it?" he replied.

Constance's father gave a gruff, huff in response. He obviously assumed everyone in London society knew who he was, and his exalted status.

Rude ignorant prick. Just because one of your ancestors was in the good books of a king doesn't make you any better than me.

He thought for a moment before reluctantly offering his hand. If he was going to court the man's daughter, then concessions had to be made.

The hairs on the back of his neck prickled when Mister Harforde hesitated. The limp handshake the gentleman eventually stooped to offer him, was so poor that it could only be seen for what it likely was, an intended slight. Monsale was quickly beginning to form a solid dislike of Mister Harforde.

What did Naomi say about the daughter? The father runs her life.

Miss Constance and Mrs. Harforde remained several feet adrift of them. Neither moved an inch. It was clear that Mister Harforde was taking the measure of his potential son-in-law, before deciding whether Monsale was worthy of meeting his daughter.

Why the devil did Kitty put this girl's name on the list?

Mister Harforde moved toward a spot a little away from the rest of the gathering and Monsale reluctantly followed. Constance and Mrs. Harforde remained where they were, staring down their noses at anyone who happened to pass them by.

As soon as they were out of earshot of other guests, Constance's father wasted no time in getting to the point. He stood, hands behind his back and considered Monsale over the top of his spectacles.

"I am not certain of you Monsale. I have heard rumors of you and your shady dealings. And I don't like the sound of them. My Constance will not be married off to some bestial rogue, even if he does have a title."

Bestial rogue? Actually, that sounds rather appealing. I should try that as my new moniker.

He opened his mouth, ready to reply, but Mister Harforde continued. "The Duchess of Redditch had some kind words to say about you, which to be honest is the first time I have heard anyone call you a good man. From what I understand, you have led an interesting life. What do you have to say for yourself?"

Monsale stifled a laugh. He knew exactly what an interesting life meant.

Oh, you don't know the half of it.

He cleared his throat. "I have experienced many things during my three and thirty years, Mister Harforde. I will grant you that, but so have many other men."

He got a haughty derisive snort in reply. "Yes, well, they are not the ones looking to secure the hand of my sweet Constance. I tell you here and now that I won't let her be taken in marriage by a blackguard. Or the son of one. Wasn't your father some sort of pirate? And then your uncle died under mysterious circumstances in the West Indies. Disgraceful business."

After mentally putting a line through Constance's name, Monsale dropped all pretense at good manners.

"Bermuda. Not the West Indies. You may wish to avail yourself of a map, sir. And yes, my father was a full-blown, unashamed pirate. As was I from the time I could wield a pistol. And there was nothing mysterious about the death of my uncle. He died in my arms when I was but thirteen years of age. Shot by a slave trader in Cable Bay."

"Well, I never…"

Monsale leaned in close and touched a finger to the glass of Mister Harforde's spectacles, pushing them back on his face. This action left a pleasing mark on the lens, through which the gentleman now glared back at him.

"I don't suppose you have done anything of interest in

your life. Which goes a long way to explaining why you are such a weasel of a man. Have no fear Mister Harforde, I won't be troubling your daughter. Good evening, sir."

Leaving a blustering Harforde in his wake, Monsale made for the door.

One down, two to go.

❧

Arriving home, he arranged to send a note to Kitty informing her of the evening's progress, or rather lack thereof. Naomi had been right in her judgement of the Harforde family. For a brief moment, he pondered whether she might have been the better choice to put the list of potential brides together, but then thought the better of it.

Why Naomi's name wasn't on the list still had him stumped.

Is she really that angry with me?

Inside the front door of Monsale House, he was greeted by Adan. His steward's face reflected his own disappointment. If things had gone well with Constance, he wouldn't be home so early.

"Can I take it that the first lady was not suitable?" asked Adan.

"I don't know. I didn't get to meet her. But the three minutes I spent with her pompous father was more than enough."

His thoughts of this evening's failure were suddenly pushed aside as the unmistakable hint of perfume reached his nose. Monsale sniffed and Adan's scowl transformed into a bright smile.

"Yes, your grace, they have arrived."

Monsale hurried to the entrance of the ballroom and flung open the doors. He was greeted with a sight which had him grinning from ear to ear.

Four large wooden crates had been stacked in the middle of the floor. One had been opened and several large pots with pink flowers were visible inside. It was from these blooms that the heady scent emanated. Monsale rushed across the floor, giddy as a child on Christmas morning, dropping to his knees in front of the first pot.

"Oh, damask roses. Aren't they beautiful? So delicate and yet, their scent fills the room."

Adan came to stand next to the box. "They are rather lovely. We have only had time to check this first crate, but they all seem to have arrived in good condition."

His long-serving steward was but one of a select number of people who understood what the roses meant to Monsale.

Memories of his late mother were few and vague. The clearest of them, was an image frozen in time, of her standing next to a rose bush in the garden of their house in Bermuda. He could still recall her words as she bent and held her face close to a perfectly formed damask bloom, smiling as she inhaled its wonderful perfume.

"Andrew, roses always bring me joy," she said.

On the morning that Sarah McNeal died, James had gone into the yard and ripped out the rose bushes with his bare hands, laying waste to what had once been a perfect garden. The young Andrew dumbstruck with grief, watched helplessly as his father destroyed every last bloom.

The only thing which remained of the roses were some dry, pressed petals in a diary left to Monsale by his mother.

By having these rose bushes shipped from Morocco he was able to relive those precious memories once more. Of a time when he still had a family. Before it all went to hell.

Getting to his feet, he carefully lifted the pot. Tonight, he would be sleeping with it on the table next to his bed. Tomorrow the Monsale House servants would begin planting the mature bushes in the garden, the younger plants finding a place in the glass hothouse.

"Well at least this evening wasn't a complete waste of time," he said.

Adan cleared his throat. "I hate to interrupt your joy, but may I ask about your grace's plans for the next young lady on the list? Time is not something we have to spare."

Monsale continued to stare at the pretty pink blooms. Nothing, not even this evening's unpleasant encounter with the Harforde's, could diminish his delight at the safe arrival of the newest members of his floral collection.

Adan, of course, was right, the roses were wonderful, but he had to address the issue of finding a bride. By August twenty-fourth Monsale had to have a wife by his side as he knelt in front of the Prince Regent.

"We need to continue with the search. So, tomorrow I shall endeavor to meet with the second prospective bride on the list. But rather than try to meet the young lady and her parents at a formal gathering, I want to invite them here for supper. Let them see the house and what marrying a duke will bring to their fortunes."

"Very good your grace. You could even show them your roses."

A soft smile sat on Monsale's lips. Everyone loved flowers. A wife who shared his appreciation of roses would be a plus.

"I shall, thank you, Adan. Tell the staff to wait until after tomorrow evening to plant the bushes. In the meantime, I want the roses all carefully removed from the crates and set about the ballroom."

He marched upstairs, pot in hand and headed for his bedroom. By inviting the next potential bride to his home, he might get a chance to speak to her. To learn more about the young woman.

His married friends had always pressed the need for a couple to have shared interests. Something with which to build a relationship upon, and also to provide common ground on which husband and wife could meet when times were tough.

A wife who appreciates roses would be a perfect match.

At the entrance to his bedroom Monsale stopped. A frown creased his brow. Even he was aware that marriage was more than just meeting the obligation of an oath to the crown. Soon a woman would inhabit this house. She would sleep in his bed. Share his life.

He would have a wife.

"I have no idea how to be a husband," he muttered.

Nor did he have a clue as to what he would do when his bride inevitably uncovered the secrets of his dirty business dealings. Mister Harforde had it wrong; an interesting life was the least of Monsale's problems.

He had a dark past. And what woman would want to give her heart to such an unscrupulous rogue?

Chapter Seven

E*leven Days to go.*

"Have you heard from Monsale?" asked Naomi, popping her head around the door of her mother's sitting room.

It was late morning and Naomi had held off for as long as she could. She was desperate to discover how things between Monsale and Miss Constance Harforde had gone the previous evening.

Kitty lifted her gaze from the note which sat open on her desk. She beckoned for her daughter to enter. Naomi, hands behind her back and fingers crossed, stepped into the room. Her eyes flitted to the paper, then back to her mother's pensive face.

"I received this missive from Monsale House just over an hour ago. Apparently, Mister Harforde treated Monsale like he was a dirty interloper. Said some very unkind things about his father. Accused him of being a pirate. Needless to say, Constance is off the list."

Doing her best to hide her delight at this news, Naomi

adopted a thoughtful study to her demeanor. "Well, I suppose Mister Harforde was correct. James McNeal *was* a pirate. Isn't that why his brother sailed to Bermuda? The duke was coming to take custody of the young Andrew, to save him from a life of villainy."

Kitty sighed. "Naomi, we do not ever discuss the details of Monsale's provenance, even at home. Why your father foolishly trusted you with that secret, I shall never understand."

Because he saw the effect Monsale had on me the moment we met.

Lady Naomi Steele might have been but a girl, but the attraction was instantaneous. Unlike her mother, the Duke of Redditch wasn't blind to his daughter's infatuation with the orphaned Andrew McNeal. Her father had told her the truth of Monsale's past as soon as she reached a marriageable age. She suspected his logic to be one of, the more you know about the devil, the less chance you have of eloping with him.

Kitty may well think she had the right of it when it came to the full extent of Monsale's sordid past, but it was nothing to what her daughter knew of his more recent exploits. And while Harry had let more salacious details slip over the years, Naomi had also made a point of filling in as many of the gaps as she could herself.

Her father might have hoped his advice had deterred her from any thoughts of loving Monsale, but it had had quite the opposite effect. She was steadfast in her love for the leader of the rogues of the road. Determined that she would one day be his wife. That he would freely offer her his love.

And how well is that plan going?

The issue of the other ladies on her mother's list was her main concern this morning. If she could overcome that obstacle, Monsale would be forced to reconsider his options.

"Such a pity about Constance. Oh, well. That leaves only two names on the list. Who is next and when is Monsale going to meet with her?"

And how soon can I strike her name off the list?

"Lady Miriam Shadbolt. Monsale is going to host the Shadbolt family at his home this evening," replied Kitty.

The titter at hearing Miriam Shadbolt's name, died instantly on Naomi's lips. He had invited people to dine at Monsale House?

Monsale never has guests at his home. I have known him since I was a child, and I've never been allowed to set foot in the place. And now he has…

She hadn't seen this coming.

Think. What do you know about Miriam Shadbolt, apart from her being a dullard?

Her smile crept back to her face. She knew plenty about the Shadbolt family. And had heard all the sordid rumors. Many of which she knew to be true.

"The Shadbolt family was an odd choice Mama. You know their reputation about the *ton* is almost as bad as Monsale's."

"Desperate times call for desperate measures. There are far fewer families in town at the moment than I had thought there were. And while the Shadbolt's are known to be a little tight with their blunt, they are a perfectly acceptable *ton* family. And, you shouldn't be making those sorts of remarks about Monsale," tutted Kitty.

It took all of Naomi's strength to hide her utter delight knowing Miriam *Grasping* Shadbolt was next on the list. She had no doubt that Monsale would find the money hungry family distasteful. He might well be the financial genius that Harry had whispered he was, but she knew Monsale wasn't one for engaging in any sort of discussion about the crass subject of money.

What did have her concerned, however, was the haste at which he was moving in his search for a wife. Three days, and already he was almost halfway through the list. By the end of today, there was every chance that only one name would remain.

I have to make certain that lady number two is out of the running, then focus on the last one.

If she was going to bring Monsale to his knees, and have him pleading for her hand in marriage, she had better move fast.

"So, what are your plans for the day?" asked her mother.

"I am going to visit Alice and baby Jonathan this morning, then do a spot of shopping. After that, I might just come home and stay in for the rest of the day. There aren't any entertainments or parties of note on offer tonight."

Kitty folded up Monsale's letter with a sigh. "Are you sure you don't want to add your name to the list? I am certain Monsale would have no objection."

Naomi shook her head. His having no objection was the root of the problem. She wasn't going to be made to feel honored at being considered for the position of his wife.

He is going to fight for me. If he won't, then we are destined never to wed.

Her parents had been happily married for many years. Like any other couple, they had their moments of disagreements, but there was passion, commitment, and love evident between them. And she wanted to see the same glint of desire shining in Monsale's eyes whenever he looked at her, as she saw when her father cast his gaze lovingly over Kitty.

I want to be wanted. And for him to ache for my love.

"Thank you, Mama, but I am firmly set on my decision. I am not going on the list, and the sooner Monsale gets that through his thick skull the better."

Kitty rose from her writing desk and came to embrace her. She pulled Naomi into a warm, motherly hug. "I don't know what you think you are playing at my girl, but I must caution you, this is not a game. By the end of this week, Monsale will have chosen his bride. A wedding shall no doubt be conducted as swiftly after that as can be arranged. If you want to be the woman to whom he is standing next to in front of the priest, then be very careful about your next move."

Pulling out of her mother's arms, Naomi placed a tender kiss on Kitty's cheek.

"Thank you, Mama. I think I have the measure of him. And if I don't, then I only have myself to blame. I shall give your love to Alice and the baby."

Chapter Eight

E*leven Days to go.*
That evening.

Monsale fussed with the edges of his cravat. His fingers were on the lapels of his jacket, straightening them, when he suddenly stopped. He scowled at himself in the bedroom mirror.

What the hell am I doing? I don't preen. And I most certainly don't fuss.

Guests were a rarity at Monsale House; so rare that the head butler had checked twice when he was given directions to arrange a formal supper for this evening. Apart from the other members of the RR Coaching Company, Monsale didn't ever host anyone in his home.

His upbringing had left him with a deep-seated mistrust of people. That he himself was one of the least trustworthy people in London only added to his social discomfort. Harry, George, Gus, and Stephen understood him. And while they too didn't share everything with Monsale, at least they were open about it.

It was an unspoken understanding among the five of them, that Monsale always took an extra secret cut out of the proceeds from their business dealings. This was a world he understood. The search for a wife had him sailing into uncharted waters.

Worry about the future sat constantly in his mind. Marriage involved more than simply solving the issue of the fealty oath to the Prince of Wales. His thoughts kept circling back to the same list of problems. Being married, meant having a wife. A woman who would expect to live in this house, to have visitors. And children.

He stood on the cusp of a momentous life change. One for which he wasn't the least prepared.

"But if I don't go through with a wedding, I will lose it all," he muttered.

Over the years he had been able to successfully keep his dodgy dealings and at times outright illegal activities a secret by not allowing other people into his private space. Monsale House was his fortress, its high walls and doors kept the world firmly locked out.

A tap on the bedroom door, had him sighing. "Come in."

Adan appeared. "Your grace. Lord and Lady Shadbolt's carriage has just drawn up in the rear mews."

Why does it feel like there are enemies at the gate of my castle?

His steward didn't usually announce arrivals, not that there were many of them, but Monsale had been clear in his instructions. Adan was to ensure that the guests spent their time this evening in the foyer, the dining room, and nowhere else. But just in case, All RR Coaching Company business papers had been secured under lock and key. His secrets were kept hidden and safe.

Monsale himself, had wandered into the odd study or two while attending a party at a private residence, serendipitously coming across valuable information contained in papers which had been left lying about the place by a careless host.

Visitors to Monsale House would not be afforded the same opportunity.

"Thank you, Adan."

From out of his jacket pocket, Adan produced a folded up and sealed note. He handed it to Monsale. "This arrived a short time ago. The footman said he had strict instructions to make sure it was delivered promptly to you, along with the request that it be read immediately."

Monsale took the missive and turned it over. He frowned at the crest on the wax seal. It was the Duke of Redditch's household mark. Breaking the seal, he opened the letter.

Notes on Lady Miriam Shadbolt.
Not much to say about her in particular, but the Shadbolt family are obsessed with money. They will do anything to save a farthing. Make sure any trinkets of value are well out of sight, otherwise you may never see them again.

The note was unsigned, but he could hazard a good guess as to who had sent it. Naomi was continuing in her role of list assistant. He screwed it up and handed it back to Adan. "Go and check the dining room. Move those delicate porcelain miniatures that are on the sideboard and look for anything else that could be easily slipped into a jacket pocket."

Adan raised an eyebrow. "Light fingered guests?"

Monsale gave a hum of displeasure. "Apparently so."

He headed downstairs and stood in the foyer ready to greet potential bride number two and her parents.

Monsale was relieved to discover that unlike Mister Harforde, Lord and Lady Shadbolt at least knew their manners. The viscount bowed low to Monsale, then introduced his wife and daughter. Lady Miriam dipped into a comfortable curtsy.

"Your grace, it is a pleasure to meet you. And thank you so much for inviting us to dine with you this evening," she said.

Not bad. She can string two words of conversation together without too much effort. I expect she could manage to play hostess at a dinner party and not make a mess of things.

A quick study of the girl revealed an ordinary looking young woman. She wasn't beautiful, but neither was she plain. Her long chestnut hair was set in a simple, but elegant chignon. Her matching eyes held a glint of intelligence. Lady Miriam might not stir his blood, but he could appreciate why Kitty had thought to include her on the list.

Monsale escorted Lady Shadbolt into the dining room, while Miriam and her father followed. It was then that the whispers began.

"Look at that rug, Miriam, I bet that cost a pretty penny."

"You did say he was seriously rich," replied Miriam.

Doing his utmost to ignore the less than subtle conversation that continued on between father and daughter, Monsale was stunned when Lady Shadbolt turned from admiring a nearby painting and boldly inquired. "Is that a Reynolds? What sort of money do you think it would fetch on the open market?"

"I…I have no idea," he stammered.

At the dining table the footmen pulled out the chairs for the ladies. Lady Shadbolt's gaze ran along the length of the highly polished surface. She turned to her husband and Monsale caught a breathy "Chippendale, worth a small fortune."

His heart sank. Naomi had been right; the Shadbolt's were obsessed with money.

After taking their seats, the first course of the evening was placed in front of them. The fresh salmon was beautifully presented. The kitchen had spared no expense or effort. He couldn't find it in his heart to begrudge the Monsale House chef for the extravagance. The poor man spent most of his days creating gastronomic delights which the staff only ever ate. A generous salary and the luster of working for a duke likely the only thing which kept him in Monsale's service for the past five years. Tonight, would have been a welcome change for the chef.

When Lady Shadbolt picked up her knife and examined the hallmarks on the side, Monsale didn't know where to look. Lady Miriam wasn't any better. She lifted her McNeal family crested dinner plate and looked at the underside of it. "Spode. More money wasted."

For the first time in his life, Monsale found himself embarrassed by someone else's behavior. His gaze flittered over the table, to a fine pair of silver salt and pepper shakers.

I had better keep an eye on those just in case Lord Shadbolt takes a fancy to them.

He turned to speak to the viscount, halting mid-move when out of the corner of his eye, he caught sight of Lady Shadbolt picking up the saltshaker and dropping it casually into her reticule.

"So Monsale, how many rooms does this house have? And more importantly which ones will you be allocating to my good lady wife and I once you and our dear Miriam are wed?"

It took a long slow blink for Monsale to find the right words with which to respond.

"I wasn't expecting you to come and live here. Don't you have your own townhouse in Margaret Street?" he replied.

The viscount mumbled something under his breath, then answered. "Yes, but we figured we could save a penny or three by coming to live here. It makes perfect sense. Costs a fortune to heat our house."

"Not to mention the outrageous wages that our servants demand that we pay them," added Lady Shadbolt.

Monsale did a double take as he realized the pepper shaker was now also gone from the table. Lady Shadbolt had lightning quick fingers.

The cheek of these people. You invite them to supper, and they steal your possessions right from under your nose.

He could just imagine what it would be like if he did marry their daughter. There was every chance that he would come home from the RR Coaching Company one night to discover they had stripped the place bare and sold everything.

Lady Shadbolt pointed at her daughter. "Make sure you eat everything on your plate my dear. That way you won't be hungry when we get home."

"Yes Mama."

"We could always get the kitchen staff here to pack us some food to take when we leave. I am sure they have plenty to spare," replied Lord Shadbolt.

Who are these people?

He was mortified. Which for Monsale, was saying something. This was a man who had stolen a ship right from under the noses of the French navy, then sailed past their largest warship and bared his ass at the vice-admiral on deck.

Damn it. I am not going to sit here and be picked over like a bloody carcass.

"I'm afraid there won't be any extra food, the servants will have eaten it all within the hour," he replied.

Think yourselves lucky I haven't thrown you out.

Lord Shadbolt grumbled something about always asking for a large plate of food to take home whenever he dined at friend's houses, but Monsale pretended not to hear.

He had already heard more than enough. Lady Miriam's name was about to come off the list. But not before he'd had some fun at the expense of his obnoxious guests.

"You were asking about moving in here. I am afraid I have no spare rooms. What with the orphans who come to stay over the summer. Then there are my many friends who also live here on a semi-permanent basis. Miriam and I simply won't be able to accommodate you."

"Orphans. How many do you host?" replied Lord Shadbolt.

Monsale counted on his fingers. "Nine, though if all the triplets decide to come, we could have an even dozen."

Lord and Lady Shadbolt exchanged a look of grave disappointment which only served to encourage Monsale.

Time to twist the knife in a little more.

"My friend Augustus Jones, stayed here for many weeks earlier this year. Just about ate me out of house and home. He and his new French wife will likely use Monsale House as their base when they visit London."

"These guests will pay you for room and board, won't they?" asked Lord Shadbolt.

The worry in his voice had Monsale curling his toes up in his boots with delight.

"Of course not. I would never ask my friends for money. Actually, that is not entirely true. I have been known to put my hand out when I need their help in settling my gambling debts."

He chuckled and gave the viscount a cheeky wink. "Bit of a loss when it comes to the cards. I can never keep up with what I am supposed to hold and what I should be throwing away."

Lord Shadbolt turned a whiter shade of pale. "But you are one of the richest men in all of England."

Monsale moved in for the kill. He screwed up his face. "On paper, yes. But…"

"But what?" exclaimed Lady Shadbolt.

"If you deduct the amount of money, I owe my creditors and the bank you will find there actually isn't much left. To be frank with you, I was kind of hoping young Miriam's dowry would see some of the more pressing creditors away from my doorstep for a time. After that, who knows. We may well have to go and live in a cheaper part of town. Or even move in with you."

Lord Shadbolt pushed back his chair and got to his feet. His wife and daughter did the same. "So, what you are saying is that you are flimsy with your money?"

Monsale remained seated. "Steady on old chap. It's not entirely my fault that everything in this house is mortgaged."

He waved a hand grandly about in the air. "It doesn't really matter that one day the bank will probably come and take the carpets, the furniture, likely even the salt and pepper shakers. As long as Miriam and I are happy that's what truly counts. Don't you agree?"

The Shadbolt's moved as one toward the door and out into the foyer. Lord Shadbolt bellowed for his carriage to be made ready for their departure. "We are leaving immediately."

He turned to Monsale, slowly shaking his head. "You and my daughter would never suit. Thank you for this evening. Good night, your grace."

Lady Miriam hurried to her father's side. "But Papa, you said he was the one. He had deep pockets."

Her father put an arm around his daughter's shoulder. "Don't you fret my dear. Papa will find you a rich, elderly baron to marry. With luck, he won't have more than a few years in him and once he has slipped off you will be set up for life."

Monsale painted a pained and disappointed expression on his face. But inside he was dancing a jig of glee. As the Monsale House butler escorted the guests out, Adan stepped into the foyer.

"That ended rather early and abruptly, your grace. The

second course is yet to be served. Didn't they enjoy the food?"

He shook his head slowly. "More like Lord and Lady Shadbolt didn't appreciate the size of my bank account. Told them I had a few financial problems which their daughter's dowry might help to alleviate. When they discovered that I wasn't flush with money, they couldn't get out of here fast enough."

Adan snorted. As he had been overseeing the accounts for many years, the steward knew to the exact penny how much was in both the official and secret bank accounts of the Monsale estate.

"That reminds me. You will need to make a trip to Garrard's in the morning and order a new set of silver salt and pepper shakers. We appear to have misplaced some this evening."

"The nerve," muttered Adan.

The table pieces were easily replaced. And while he had been fortunately spared from a life of forever keeping a wary eye on his light-fingered in-laws, Monsale was still without a wife.

Two down, one to go.

One name was now left on the list. All his hopes pinned on a woman he had never met and who might just transpire to be as terrible an option, or god forbid worse, as the first two had been.

And all of this because Naomi is too bloody stubborn to throw her hat in the ring.

If she could just see her way to bend a little, give him but an inch, he might still be able to save the Monsale title and fortune.

Some things are easier said than done.

Chapter Nine

T*en Days to go.*
Redditch House, Grosvenor Street

Excitement bubbled in Naomi's stomach. Tonight, Gus and Evangeline Jones would get to celebrate their recent marriage with his English friends and family. The couple had been wed in France earlier in the year but had decided to delay their wedding party until their arrival in London.

Having met the charming Evangeline earlier in the week, Naomi could well understand why Gus had left his country to start a new life with her in Brittany. The French beauty was certainly captivating.

Her own delight in hearing the news that Lady Miriam Shadbolt was not going to be the new Duchess of Monsale also added to Naomi's buoyant mood. There was only one name now left on the list of potential brides. One woman who stood between her and having Monsale finally admit his mistake and beg for her hand in marriage.

Tonight however, she was going to do her best to set aside all worries of the tall, brown-haired noble who constantly teased and tempted her. This was Evangeline and Augustus Jones's night to shine.

Just avoid him. Find ways to keep busy. See if Mama needs anything. Mingle and chat with friends and family.

And if all that failed, she could always rely on the time-honored female weapon of choice— a convenient headache. One which would see her retire early to her room. Monsale was not going to spoil her evening.

Making her way downstairs to the elegant main ballroom of her home, she was the picture of a young woman without a care in the world. No one would ever suspect that it was taking every ounce of her courage to maintain her composure.

Monsale of course would be among the guests at the ball this evening. With the Jones family home being too small to hold such a gathering, Lord and Lady Steele had graciously offered to host the wedding celebrations for Gus and Evangeline at Redditch House.

Dutiful daughter that she was, Naomi came and stood alongside her mother and father as they welcomed the arriving guests.

I am like an ice queen. Serene and untouchable.

She kept this mantra going in her head, fearful that if someone did actually lay a hand on her, she may well shatter.

Jane and George Hawkins were the first to arrive, followed by Alice and Harry. They had just said a quick hello before Bridget and Stephen joined the gathering.

"Naomi, I do love your gown," said Bridget.

They exchanged a brief hug. Naomi gave her new dress a twirl. "I had this made for the social season, but never quite found the right occasion for which to debut it."

She had thought to cleverly accessorize the red and white striped gown with a dark blue Spencer, as a salute to Evangeline's home country, but Kitty had suggested that might be a touch unpatriotic at a London social event. In the end she had left the gown without a jacket or Spencer, relying on a cotton chemise to keep her warm. In her hair she wore a small headband decorated with fresh red roses.

Bridget leaned in close. "Is Monsale here yet? I heard his search for a bride is not going all that well."

"No, he isn't here as yet. We expect him any minute. The first two ladies on the list are both gone, which means he is fast running out of options," replied Naomi, keeping her expression placid.

Only time would tell if Monsale changed his strategy.

"Are you going to make a move?" asked Bridget.

Having finally found happiness, her friend was clearly desperate for Naomi to also share in the joy of wedded bliss. "No. I am not. He can come to me," replied Naomi.

The front door of Redditch House opened once more. Gus's parents, Captain, and Mrs. Jones were announced. They gave a cheery wave to everyone, then quickly stepped aside.

An excited murmur rippled through the gathering, followed by applause as Gus and Evangeline stepped inside the foyer.

Naomi held her hands together as emotion welled up inside her. Evangeline, the blushing bride, was dressed in a cream gown, with dark pink bows embroidered on both the bodice and the skirt. In her pale, blonde hair she wore a matching pink ribbon.

"Absolutely stunning," Naomi whispered.

She and Bridget exchanged happy grins. Her gaze had just turned back to the newlyweds, when Monsale stepped through the doorway. He appeared embarrassed at having arrived after the guests of honor, moving quickly around to come and stand alongside Jane and George. Naomi caught a curt. "You are late Monsale," from Jane.

Jane Hawkins hadn't grown up in London society and never appeared intimidated by the likes of nobility, especially the Duke of Monsale. George's wife was the perfect foil for her reformed thief of a husband. She didn't suffer fools gladly.

"Yes, sorry. Last-minute snag, with my solicitor and the marriage settlements. I had to dash here on foot from Mount Street," he replied.

Naomi shot Bridget a sideways glance. Watching Monsale be put in his place by a mere female was always great sport. The fact that Jane was heavy with child, only added to the fun.

With the guests, all now having arrived, the gathering moved into the main dining room. Gus and Evangeline sat with Captain and Mrs. Jones either side of them. Mrs. Jones paid particular attention to her daughter-in-law, constantly making sure that she was eating properly and was able to understand the conversation.

Naomi found herself seated with Alice on one side, and Sir Stephen Moore on the other. She silently cursed her mother for having placed Monsale directly across the table from her. Every time she lifted her gaze, she met his mischievous gray eyes.

After the third time their eyes met, and she caught the hint of a smile on the edge of his mouth, Naomi decided to focus on her soup. Chicken and vegetable broth was a safer option than being teased by a man who seemed intent on vexing her this evening.

When the speeches and main course were finally done a weary hour later, she was one of the first people to rise from the table and head toward the ballroom.

Thank heavens that is over. If I had to sit opposite Monsale for another minute I think I might have committed murder.

She took a deep fortifying breath as she stepped into the room. Her parents had spared no expense with the evening. Cream and pink paper lanterns were draped across the ceiling corner to corner. There were also several large vases filled with pink roses lining the far wall of the ballroom.

I wonder if they were a gift from Monsale, he does so love his flowers.

A small orchestra had set up at one end of the room, and the gentle 'plink' of violins being tuned drifted to her ears.

A hand slipped under her arm and Naomi found a grinning Evangeline standing beside her. "This looks wonderful. People have been so welcoming and kind, I shall find it almost impossible to return home to France."

Naomi placed her hand gently over Evangeline's. "I think that's the idea. If you fall in love with London, you may want to stay."

Evangeline laughed. "If only. But we have the château to continue rebuilding, and the shipping business is always calling for Gus's attention. Occupé. Occupé."

Naomi didn't reply. She doubted that there was a person in the room who didn't know that the *shipping business* was actually a smuggling operation, moving goods between Brittany and Portsmouth. She was tempted to ask Evangeline what her plans for the future were with regard to the illegal trade. Bridget had made mention of Gus wanting to find another source of income, one which was less dangerous. There was hope that in time all the members of the RR Coaching Company would finally step away from their old lives.

And that thought raised another question in her mind.

What will Monsale do when he takes on a wife? He can't think to keep that sort of thing secret for too long.

The first strains of a quadrille now filled the room. Bridget and Stephen, paired up with Harry and Alice. The Jones's and Lord and Lady Steele making up the rectangular set of dancers.

Naomi frowned. Why weren't the newlywed couple being included? Across the other side of the dance floor, Gus was conducting an animated conversation with George and Monsale.

"You are not dancing?"

Evangeline shook her head. "I don't know the steps of your English dances. I can muddle my way through a French traditional folk dance, such as the *gavotte* but the waltz and this formation dancing is beyond me. I might come from a good family, but with the upheaval in my country which followed the revolution, dancing lessons were a luxury not afforded to me."

The heat of embarrassment burned on Naomi's cheeks. She didn't know much about Evangeline's background, but it appeared to have been less privileged than her own.

"I'm sorry, that was thoughtless of me. Sometimes I forget that not all my friends have been granted the sort of life I have led," she said.

Evangeline waved her concerns away. "You have all been so welcoming, I cannot begin to tell you how much that means to me. Besides, I have Gus and my home, it's more than I ever thought I would have."

Naomi beckoned a footman over and selected a glass of champagne, handing it to Evangeline. She took one for herself, and they sipped their drinks. It was nice to simply watch friends and family enjoying themselves.

A short while later, the tempo of the evening changed as the orchestra struck up a waltz. The different ways the various couples moved around the floor was interesting. Harry and Alice laughed their way through the steps, with Harry throwing in the occasional outrageous piece of footwork. Alice was in fits of giggles.

He will always be a society peacock at heart.

The sensual movements of Stephen and Bridget had Naomi taking several hurried, and large gulps of her champagne. They didn't seem to give a damn if anyone else saw their love. When Stephen captured his wife's lips in a scorching kiss as he pulled her through a turn, Naomi didn't know where to look.

Gosh. That is…

Her skin flushed with heat. As she tore her gaze from the dance floor, she met the cool gray eyes of —him. Monsale glanced at the orchestra, then leaned in and spoke to Gus. There was a brief exchange, at the end of which Monsale nodded. His eyes shifted back to Naomi, then to the dancers, before returning to her once more.

He is thinking of dancing, that would be…no. Don't you dare, Naomi Steele. You swore you would never again ask him to dance. He has humiliated you for the last time.

Their gazes were still locked on one another as Monsale made his way across the floor. He was headed straight for her. She hated the way her heart began to beat fast in her chest as he approached.

If he asks you to dance, be calm and polite. Hold your nerve. And for heaven's sake, don't appear eager or grateful. If only my heart would stop racing.

He didn't deserve her going all weak-at-the-knees just because he finally decided that it was time to take her hand and dance.

Monsale drew closer.

And take a deep breath.

She caught the salacious grin on his lips and silently cursed him; his swagger only made things worse. The blackguard.

Her heart rate kicked up to an almost scary pace, going 'thump, thump' in her chest. Despite her best endeavors, hope flared. She had been waiting years for this moment.

When he reached her, he nodded. "Lady Naomi. Madame Jones. I trust you ladies are enjoying this evening."

To her surprise and outraged dismay, he then kept going. Gliding past them without missing a step.

Evangeline clearly oblivious to the simmering undercurrent of the exchange, smiled sweetly at Monsale. "Your grace.

Tonight, has been wonderful. And thank you for the generous gift of the roses, they are beautiful."

A heated volcano of rage flared up inside Naomi. There could be no mistaking what Monsale had just done. She glanced down at her glass, furious that she had finished her champagne. If she hadn't, she would have thrown the drink in his face.

You dirty rotten tease.

As Monsale continued on his way, his gaze shifted to George and Jane. He held up a hand and gave them a cheery greeting. "Ah, just the people I was wishing to speak to, do you have a minute?"

"Excuse me Evangeline, I must attend to an urgent matter," said Naomi, her voice quaking with fury.

With her teeth sunk firmly into her bottom lip, Naomi spun on her heel and marched toward the door. An attending footman barely caught the champagne glass as she thrust it into his hands. She couldn't get out of the ballroom fast enough. Any moment now she was going to explode.

Chapter Ten

Naomi made it most of the way out of the ballroom and along the adjoining hall before the pounding of heavy boots had her looking back over her shoulder. Monsale was bearing down on her at a furious rate.

He didn't bother to speak, rather he seized Naomi by the arm and dragged her into the nearest room, closing the door firmly behind him. To her surprise, he locked it.

"What the devil are you playing at?" she exclaimed.

"You are the one who seems to think this is all a game. What I want to know is when are you going to stop? There is only one name left on the list, and it's not yours," huffed Monsale.

Naomi yanked her arm out of his hold and stepped away. She needed distance between her and Monsale. More for his safety than anything.

How dare he come in here and accuse her of being a tease. "You asked Mama to prepare a list of women who might want to marry you. My name is not on it because I chose not to be included."

He took several quick steps toward her, grinning when Naomi didn't flinch. Most other women might be intimidated by such a move, but she certainly wasn't. And any attempt on his part to tower over her, was also doomed to fail. She wasn't short of stature for a female, with the top of her head being level with his nose.

"Stubborn. Bull-headed. Intractable," he ground out.

She narrowed her eyes at him. "I think you mean pig-headed. And you forgot determined."

"Determined to be what?"

Damn. I shouldn't have said that word. I meant willful.

Taking a deep breath, she gathered her wits.

"Determined not to be a weak female who can be pushed around by someone like you. I know what you were doing just now in the ballroom, you seek to put me in my place. To have me begging you yet again for a dance, all the while knowing you will refuse. Well, I am done with you dangling that rotten carrot in front of me, and then whipping it away. You think just because you are a duke, and therefore top of the pile that I should yield. I would rather remain on the shelf and..."

He suddenly leaned in, his gaze settling briefly on the fresh roses in her hair. His deep growl sent a bolt of lust through Naomi's body. It settled between her legs, where it lingered and pulsed. She blinked slowly, doing her utmost not to reveal what this was doing to her. How aroused she had suddenly become.

Monsale inched closer. They were now closer than they had ever been before. She caught the hint of his gentleman's cologne. Warmed by his skin, it held a dark, musky allure. Primal urges stirred in her veins.

Her heart danced to a quick pitter-patter beat as she stared helplessly into his stone-gray eyes.

Closer.

"You are the most stubborn of females."

Her breath was a struggle. "I know."

Closer still.

Her gaze drifted lower and settled on his lips. So, often they were set hard, but now they were gently parted. Soft. Inviting.

Kiss me. Tell me I am the only one. That no other woman will ever hold your heart. That I have your love. You have mine.

They were teetering on the edge, one step away from a bright future together. If he confessed his love, she would gladly give him her all. Her complete surrender. He could take her here and now. She would be his to claim.

Please Monsale. You can speak to Papa tonight. You just have to fall with me.

She was a hair's breadth away from begging when a sly grin appeared on his face.

"Put your name on the list Naomi."

Bloody. Stubborn. Intractable male. Oh!

She shoved a hand hard in his chest. Cocksure dukes were the worst. Why did he have to be the one she had lost her heart to?

If I put my name on the list, then it makes me no more special than those other girls. Women who you don't give a damn about.

If he wasn't prepared to compromise, then neither was she.

"No. I can't put my name on that list. And if you don't understand why, then you don't care enough about me to make any of this worthwhile."

His smile disappeared. "You will be the death of me, Naomi. But so be it. There is still one other lady on the list. With luck, she will agree to be my duchess. To yield. And if I do marry her, you will only have yourself to blame."

Her hands turned to fists. "That's all that matters to you, isn't it? Finding a woman who will submit to your whims. One who will meekly stand by and let you run roughshod over her heart and emotions. Well, I am not that woman."

"No, you are not, but what you are asking for is impossible. Love has never been a part of this for me. I won't change.

You cannot remake a man like me. My soul was plunged into the fiery heat of a furnace, then beaten into shape long before I met you."

Disappointment stabbed at her heart. He had just declared he could never love her. The most he was prepared to offer was the role of his duchess, and the mother of his children.

"You are right Monsale, it is impossible."

She was still staring at the door long after Monsale had taken his leave.

Chapter Eleven

N*ine Days to go.*

There was something about the smell of a newborn baby that had always delighted Naomi. The fresh alluring scent that made her want to inhale deep and drink in all that innocence. Babies held an endless fascination. The promise that one day she too might be a mother.

Her close friend, Lady Bridget Moore had recently given birth to a little girl, Elizabeth Rose. Naomi spent as much time as she could at the Moore family home in Berkeley Square. It was her place of refuge.

She and Bridget were seated in the upstairs drawing room which overlooked the gardens of the square, the morning after Gus and Evangeline's wedding ball. Bridget had left the gathering early, but the dark circles under her eyes spoke of a new mother who hadn't got much sleep.

While Naomi held the baby in her arms, Bridget rested her head against the sofa, and closed her eyes.

"How is the whole Monsale looking for a wife saga going?

I didn't get a chance to speak to you last night before I left, but Stephen says Monsale was very grumpy later in the evening," said Bridget.

Naomi glanced down and addressed the baby. "The Duke of Monsale is a silly man who can't see past the end of his long handsome nose. I am sorry Elizabeth Rose, but you will no doubt soon discover that the male of the species can be a right royal pain in the ass."

The chubby faced infant blew a spit bubble in response.

Exactly my sentiments too.

"Monsale fooled me into thinking he was about to ask me to dance. When I wouldn't play his game and left the room, he followed me. He dragged me into one of the downstairs sitting rooms and then had the effrontery to accuse me of being stubborn. Me? Talk about the pot calling the kettle black. He demanded I put my name on the list, then marched off in a huff when I said no."

She didn't want to reveal to anyone what else had transpired between her and Monsale. Of the fact that she was certain he had almost broken and kissed her. Nor did she want to talk about the cold, hard words they had exchanged. The wounds of disappointment were still too raw.

"So, how many ladies are left?" replied Bridget.

"One. Lady Euphemia Marshall. I don't know a great deal about her; she doesn't spend much time in London."

Bridget scowled. "The unknown elements are always the greatest of threats. Believe me when I say I speak from bitter experience."

Bridget's late first husband had blamed her for the lack of children in their marriage and dubbed her the *Baron Baroness*. It was only after she and Sir Stephen Moore had conducted a private affair that Bridget discovered the problem had not lain with her.

"I don't understand why you refused to let Kitty put your name on the list in the first place? Stephen tells me it has infuriated Monsale no end. I expect he thought you would, and he could then just choose you."

Hot tears of frustration suddenly pricked at Naomi's eyes. No one else seemed to understand her point of view. As far as she was concerned, there shouldn't be a list. It was beyond her comprehension as to why Monsale had even considered one.

"He might well be annoyed by my refusal, but he doesn't seem to have noticed, or if he has, care that he has hurt me. And I don't just mean my pride. You of all people should know how demeaning this is for me. Monsale can't possibly be blind to the affection I feel for him."

"I see. You mean there shouldn't be a list? Monsale should have chosen you right from the outset, and his failure to do so is what has hurt you so much. Do I have the right of it?" replied Bridget.

"Yes. You know I have never wanted to take on a husband just because it was expected of me. I've seen the love that my friends and siblings have found in marriage. The way you and Stephen are together, takes my breath away. That's what I want. And if I cannot have it with Monsale, then I shall go without."

Bridget rose from her seat and came to sit beside her. Baby Elizabeth began to fuss at the sight of her mother. Naomi wisely handed the infant over.

"I know how much it tore at my heart when I told Stephen I was pregnant; and he offered to marry me, but not live under the same roof. Men are strange creatures. He thought that was acceptable but was most put out when I declined to take his surname."

Her friend's stubborn refusal to accept anything less than Sir Stephen's full and heartfelt devotion had seen the rogue finally come to his senses and declare his love to Bridget. From what Naomi had seen, they were deliriously happy with one another.

I want the same from Monsale. He can have my everything if I can have his heart.

"Why can't Monsale see what happened between you and Sir Stephen and understand that is the path to happiness? We could have the same."

Bridget sighed. "I know. But don't forget I was pregnant Naomi; Stephen didn't have the sort of choice that Monsale has with you. He was never going to walk away from me or our family. The ties that bound us together were too strong."

Bridget was right. Not only had she been carrying his child, but she had taken custody of Stephen's orphaned half-brother Toby. She had been holding all the cards.

After last night's confrontation, Naomi wasn't sure that there was much else she could do about Monsale. There was one name left on the bridal list, and she would have to hope that fate was about to finally deal her a winning hand.

She just had to find a compelling reason for him not to marry Lady Euphemia. And then be granted the miracle of him finally coming to his senses.

I'm not certain if I can pray that hard.

Chapter Twelve

"Remember to send word if you hear whispers of any developments," said Naomi, setting her cup of half-finished tea on the side table and getting to her feet.

While Bridget looked ready to fall asleep any moment, Naomi had to go home and get her hair set in time for the ball tonight. This evening Monsale was due to meet the third, and last name on the list. Lady Euphemia Marshall.

She was still in a filthy mood over his words and trickery of the previous night, so hadn't sent Monsale a note this morning with her thoughts on the earl's daughter. Unlike Constance and Miriam, Euphemia didn't have much of a profile to speak of in London society. Her parents, Lord and Lady Marshall were well-respected members of the *ton,* so Kitty had obviously based Euphemia's inclusion on the reputation of her parents.

I need something on Lady Euphemia that will render her unsuitable. But what?

Bridget stirred on the sofa and cracked open an eye. "I shall do my best to let you know if anything comes to light regarding Monsale and his plans. But you must know that my husband and his friends hold their secrets. It takes all my feminine wiles to get Stephen to tell me anything. And when he finally does succumb to my efforts, I find that talking is the last thing he wishes to do."

Heat burned on Naomi's cheeks. She had a pretty good idea of what went on between a man and woman in the marital bed, but to hear her friend mention it, had her blushing. A tinge of envy sat in her heart. Bridget had won Stephen's love.

"And besides that, I am so tired all the time at the moment, even if Stephen did make mention of Monsale and his list, there is a good chance I would be sound asleep when he did."

Bridget shifted the baby to her other shoulder and gave her daughter a gentle pat on the back. A loud burp echoed in the room.

Naomi grinned at her friend. From the happy expression on Bridget's face, motherhood was everything she had hoped it would be.

She leaned in and placed a gentle kiss on Bridget's cheek. "I am so pleased for you. If anyone deserves to find happiness, it is you, Bridget dearest."

"Do not sell yourself short Naomi. You are a catch above all other women. Just don't let your stubborn nature cost you, the man you want."

After giving baby Elizabeth Rose a final hug, Naomi took her leave. She stepped out into the narrow hallway and was headed for the front door when familiar male voices drifted to her ears. At the top of the stairs, Stephen and Monsale were saying their own farewells.

"Check on the coach driver if you get a chance to drop by Gracechurch Street in the next day. I am sure he was alright, but we need to make sure our staff are fit for work."

That was Monsale.

"I did happen to see him yesterday. He said the fall from

the roof of the coach had only left him with bruises, but I will ask again."

The other voice was Stephen.

"Alright. I had better go. I have a ball to attend this evening, and the third woman on the list to meet."

Naomi hurried to the front door as the sound of footsteps on the stairs grew louder. She didn't bother to wait for a footman to see her out, instead she reached for the handle and hastened outside.

"Naomi, tarry a moment, will you?"

Deuce. I was hoping to avoid him.

The Steele family carriage was waiting in the street, and she quickened her steps, desperate to get away. The footman barely had time to step down from the back of the coach and open the door before she was holding her hand out for him to help her climb in.

An arm suddenly appeared in front of her, followed by the imposing form of the Duke of Monsale. The footman took a hasty step back, moving out of the way.

"Thank you, I shall assist Lady Naomi," said Monsale.

With a great degree of reluctance, she accepted his offered hand. Warm fingers wrapped around hers and a jolt of heat raced down her spine. She had been in such a hurry to leave Bridget and Stephen's house that Naomi hadn't had time to put her gloves on.

She gasped. Her gaze dropped to their joined hands. Monsale was touching her. Her mind immediately filled with visions of temptation, of the long nights she had lain awake and imagined how it would feel when he ran his fingers over her naked body.

She barely noticed her feet landing on the step of the carriage as she climbed inside. The mere touch of his fingers on her bare skin had set her mind in a whirl. Naomi dropped breathlessly onto the sumptuously cushioned bench. She was still trying to catch her breath when Monsale climbed into the carriage and pulled the door shut behind him.

Quick as a flash, he tugged the blind down, blocking them from the view of anyone who happened to be walking by.

"You and I need to talk," he said. He banged his fisted hand on the roof of the carriage, and within a matter of seconds they had drawn away from the side of the street.

Naomi finally found her wits and voice. "What are you doing?"

She scurried across the other side of the bench as Monsale came and sat beside her. The more she moved away, the closer he came. In the end she found herself tucked up in the corner, with nowhere left to go.

"About this evening. This is a make-or-break moment for me. There is only one lady left on the list for me to consider," said Monsale.

"I am perfectly aware of the precariousness of your situation. And while I am sorry to hear that neither of the first two candidates were what you were looking for in a bride, none of this is actually my concern," she replied.

He shot her a dark look. "You don't look the least bit sorry, Lady Naomi. And I am certain that you consider the subject of whom I marry to be very much your business. So perhaps you might want to consider giving up the lies."

Her mouth opened on a surprised 'o'. It wasn't every day that a woman of noble birth was called a liar.

"Alright. I am not disappointed that you haven't yet found the right one. But that is not my fault. If anyone is to blame, you should look closer to home."

Monsale raised an eyebrow. "Really? I would have thought you had a great deal to do with the current bind I find myself in."

Naomi shook her head. She was not going to be forced into making any sort of concessions to his pride.

He moved closer, his muscular thigh pressing hard against

her leg. There may have been layers of clothing between them, but she sensed the heat and power in his body just the same.

Naomi closed her eyes as Monsale brushed the back of his hand over her cheek. She silently prayed.

Touch me.

The scent of his cologne now filled her senses. He was near. She dared not open her eyes for fear of meeting his. This was more dangerous than even last night had been.

A soft, warm kiss was placed on her forehead. It held the promise of a lover's benediction. She shivered when the second kiss came, this time on the bridge of her nose.

"Naomi," he whispered.

Without conscious thought, she lifted her head, offering her lips to him. Monsale brushed the mere hint of a kiss on her mouth. "Naomi."

Her eyelids flew open when he nipped on her bottom lip with his teeth. Her whole field of vision was now filled with his light gray eyes. Two stormy pools that beckoned for her to dive into them and let herself go.

His lips came down on hers once more, and he claimed her mouth. Naomi groaned. This was what she had dreamed of for countless years. One moment of perfection and the thought of where it would lead.

Naomi's lips parted as Monsale's tongue swept past them and into her mouth. For a strong, determined man, he was surprisingly gentle with his kiss.

She tasted the hints of black tea and orange preserve, a delightful combination she was willing to spend the rest of her life enjoying if given half the chance. One kiss with Monsale would never be enough.

As the kiss continued, Naomi sensed his hesitation. He was holding back, waiting for her permission to continue. Or for her to push him away.

I have waited years for this, for you to claim me. What took you so damn long?

Grasping the front of his coat, she pulled him closer, exalting when Monsale took his cue from her actions and deepened the kiss. It was time to put all those pointers about the art of kissing she had garnered from her married friends into practice.

Their tongues tangled in a frantic, messy encounter. She bit his top lip, and he withdrew. Their gazes met, a flash of passion flaring between them, before a grinning Monsale came back for more.

On and on the kiss continued. Mouths working feverishly together. Greedy for one another.

She didn't stop him, not even when he flicked the front button of her pelisse open and brushed his fingers over her peaked nipple. Her gown and light stays yielding as he pinched the bud between his finger and thumb.

Yes. Yes.

"I can just imagine how you will feel when I have you naked and beneath me. But tell me Naomi will you cry out my name when I bring you to climax, or will your mind be too muddled as your body explodes with pleasure?"

"I…I don't know. I"

She did know how it felt to come under her own hand, often imagining it was him stroking her sex. But even as the haze of lust held her in its grasp, a spark of lucid reasoning broke through.

Naomi pushed at Monsale's hand, and he released his hold. If he was lucky, he may one day find out what seeing her in the passion of her orgasm looked like; but that day was not today.

He drew back, a look of hesitation lingered momentarily on his face before his usual expression of supreme self-confidence returned.

"You know you want to experience what it would be like

to lay with me. I can read your mind. It is taking all your strength not to beg me to make you mine here and now. I know you wanted it last night," he said.

Naomi drew in a shaky breath, her body desperate to give in and claim what it craved. Her sex clenched and pulsed with need. Any moment now and she would gladly seal this deal with the devil.

"My title, my lands, and fortune would be safely out of Prinny's hands. All you have to do is put your name on the list, and start planning our wedding night," he added.

His words sent Naomi tumbling out of her lust filled fog. She punched her fist as hard as she could in the middle of his chest. A shocked, Monsale fell back. "Naomi!"

"Get off! Get away from me! You are a nothing more than a conniving swine! You will do anything to thwart the Prince of Wales, but nothing to declare your heart. This was all a wicked ploy to get me to put my name on that bloody list. What will it take to get you to understand that my answer is no?"

Her hand went straight to the roof of the carriage, and she banged loudly on it.

"Stop! Stop the carriage now!"

They both swayed as the coach veered over to the side of the street and came to a sudden halt. Naomi wasn't done. She launched herself at Monsale, fists flying. He put his hands up trying to ward her off. "Deuce woman! Stop it."

She landed a hard slap to his face just as the door of the carriage opened. The poor footman stood in the street a stunned expression on his face.

Monsale came back to her one last time, leaning in close. Their lips once more mere inches apart. "Are you insane?"

Naomi shot him a look of pure hatred. "No, but I would be if I added my name to that infernal list. There shouldn't even be a list."

Tears stung her eyes. She was certain her heart would break all over again.

"The man I marry, will have to be honest with me. To share his feelings and be open to love. Sometimes I think you are clueless when it comes to women."

Slowly shaking his head, Monsale turned away. "You are right, I haven't the foggiest. But I don't have time at my leisure to find out. If I don't marry in the next few days, I will lose it all."

He climbed out of the carriage, slamming the door deafeningly behind him. Naomi lay her head back against the soft, padded seat and covered her face with her hands.

For a brief moment, she had let herself believe he truly wanted her. That there was a chance for them to find happiness together.

"Stupid, foolish girl, why did you let him kiss you?" she muttered.

Because you have dreamed of that moment for so long. You couldn't resist temptation.

It was done. She finally knew how magnificent it was to be kissed by Monsale. Far better than anything she had ever imagined. But the price had been a sharp dagger to her heart.

Heartache at the hands of the rugged duke had been a constant for so long that at times she thought she might have become impervious to it. That she might finally be able to move on and find someone else.

Why do you torture me? What is so wrong between us that you cannot accept love?

And yet, he still held her heart, would never let it go. She was forever fated to remain tightly held in the bonds of desire.

As the carriage drew away from the side of the street once more, Naomi dried her tears and did her best to console herself.

The moment she had refused to put her name on the list,

she had set out on this road. Her determination to have Monsale finally declare the truth of his heart, the banner behind which she continued to march.

"Just have faith. Trust your instincts. He does care for me. If he didn't, then why would he be so set on me having my name on the list?"

Naomi wasn't prepared to give up. Nor did she want to try to change Monsale. She just wanted him to see that if he married for love, he could find real happiness. That having a wife who shared his heart was not something to fear. He was worthy of love.

What if the worst happens, and he does break my heart? Well, then at least I will finally know the truth. I won't waste any more years waiting.

Monsale might well be thinking he was still playing it cool with her, but his actions spoke differently. Twice in the space of one day, he had tried to cajole Naomi into doing his bidding and putting her name on his list. He was getting desperate; she could sense it.

But what would it take to finally make him concede defeat?

Chapter Thirteen

Nineteen years and many days. That's how long it had taken Monsale to finally kiss Lady Naomi Steele. To put his hands on her soft, delicious body.

For the first fifteen of those years, he hadn't viewed her as anything other than the younger sister of a friend. And if he was honest about it, for much of that time he had barely given her a second thought.

But somewhere during the years that followed, she had emerged from her cocoon and spreading her wings had magically transformed into a beautiful butterfly, right before his eyes. He couldn't see or even think about her without lust heating his soul. Burning desire for her ran deep.

Over the past year, things had become particularly problematic whenever his thoughts turned to Naomi. He wanted her. Ached for her touch.

He couldn't walk into a social event that he knew she would be attending, without automatically seeking her out. But being the damn fool that he was, the second he got near, his resolve always faltered. His only armor in this battle was his impenetrable rogue façade which he locked firmly into place. Poor Naomi was then left to deal with his cool disinterest.

It was the very reason why he didn't dance. If she saw him with another woman, Naomi would expect him to offer the same to her. The mere thought of holding her in his arms, even fully upright, sent his body into a hardened state.

But that kiss. By Jove, it was good. She didn't hold back. And those lips…

He was stuck between a rock and hard place. If Naomi behaved like any other woman, she would have immediately demanded marriage. And he would have caved and be obediently on his way over to Grosvenor Street right this very minute. There he would respectfully request an audience with the duke. After informing Naomi's father that he had just thoroughly kissed his daughter, the Duke of Redditch would agree that marriage was the only option. By the time he left Redditch House, a firm date for the wedding would have been set.

But Naomi is not like other women. She has a mind of her own. If you did go and see her father, she would never forgive you.

Monsale was still in two minds as to what he should do as he walked in the front door of his home. A somber Adan was waiting for him.

"This arrived an hour ago from Carlton House," he said.

His heart sank at the sight of the paper in his steward's hand. Where he was concerned, nothing good seemed to come out of the prince's London residence. A horrid sense of foreboding gripped him.

There is nothing to be done, but the prince's will.

Taking the letter, he broke open the seal. He sighed as he perused the contents of the note.

"He has given me a day and time for the fealty ceremony. Asked that I *RSVP* as soon as possible with the name of my good lady wife. Says it is for catering purposes only."

"Right royal little…" muttered Adan.

Screwing the letter tightly in his fist, Monsale pondered his next move. The days were rapidly ticking down. He had little over a week before he was scheduled to kneel before the Prince of Wales.

There was a long minute or two of silence, then Adan cleared his throat. "Have you considered the obvious solution to all this, your grace?" he asked.

Monsale leveled him with a sharp look. It was all he thought of from the second he woke to the time he closed his eyes.

"Yes, I have."

His father had raised him to never beg. To never give in. The family motto was *Nihil necesse est cedere.* Nothing must be yielded.

But if he failed to secure the hand of a wife and soon, he might well have to change the family coat of arms.

Lady Naomi Steele was making it all so difficult. The stubborn woman. If she didn't give in to him soon, Lady Euphemia Marshall might be his only hope.

Could I really marry a stranger?

If it meant keeping his title, and the McNeal family fortune intact, that might be precisely what he had to do.

Chapter Fourteen

N*ine Days to go.*

Naomi might well think him blind to love, but even Monsale could see the sweet looks that Lady Euphemia Marshall and Viscount Walsall exchanged whenever they thought no one else was looking. The idea of his prospective future bride already being in love with someone else sent a cold shiver down his spine.

But he was getting desperate. The letter from the Prince of Wales had been clear in its instructions. In nine days, he and his wife had to go on bended knee before the prince and swear their allegiance to the crown. For a man not used to being on his knees, Monsale was beginning to worry that it might become an uncomfortable habit.

He had stupidly thought for a moment, that the kiss he and Naomi had shared in the carriage might have changed things between them, but she steadfastly refused to come to heel.

Bloody hell. What am I going to do?

Another night, and another potential wife to meet. Monsale was down to the last girl on the list, his options rapidly shrinking. And from where he stood, across the other side of the ballroom, watching Lady Euphemia and the viscount, he had the sinking feeling that he may shortly be putting a line through her name too.

He dared not risk another evening with guests in his home. After the hasty departure of the Shadbolt family from Monsale House, and the food which had been left abandoned in the dining room, he was loathed to ask his chef to create another sumptuous meal. The current story from below stairs was that the man had taken to his bed and not stirred since.

At least he had learned some lessons from his previous encounters with the families of prospective brides. Determined not to make the same mistake he had with the Harforde's, Monsale was keen to seek out Lord and Lady Marshall as soon as he arrived. He wished to make certain of a smooth introduction to their daughter.

"Your grace."

Monsale turned as Euphemia's mother, Lady Marshall arrived at his side. She dipped into a curtsy, and he responded with a deep bow. He might well be the more senior noble, but Kitty had been clear in her instructions as to how he should behave when it came to his first meeting with Earl Marshall's wife. She was not only the daughter of a duke but had European royalty in her blood. While she was a true blueblood, to many people in London high society, he was little more than a jumped-up colonial.

Lady Marshall nodded in the direction of her daughter. "I see Euphemia has already caught your eye. She is a delightful girl. Not a beauty of the classic kind mind you, but she has an enthralling look all of her own. Always stands out in a crowd. Born to be a duchess if I do say so myself."

His gaze lingered on Lady Euphemia. She had an interesting way about her. A man would likely never tire of such a woman.

But is she the one I should marry? And what about Viscount Walsall, I am not having any starry-eyed lover sniffing around my wife's skirts.

He had to marry, but it didn't mean he was about to lower his standards. The woman he made his duchess was going to have to understand the rules of their marriage. Fidelity between him and his wife was non-negotiable.

And what about affection? Are you really going to go through with marrying someone who may just tolerate you? Or who will never freely offer you, her heart?

Tearing his gaze from Lady Euphemia, Monsale quickly scanned the room. Naomi was nowhere to be seen. She might well be content to continue playing games, but she wasn't to know how pressing time had become. And if push did finally come to shove, he wasn't going to let Prinny win.

Naomi or no, he was determined to thwart the prince regent's plans to get his hands on the Monsale title and lands.

Where are you, Naomi?

He longed to see her. To know she was alright. Her words of pain in the carriage kept rolling around in his mind. Had he pushed things too far and actually hurt her?

No. She is playing the game. The first to yield loses.

She was here somewhere; when he had spoken to Harry at the RR Coaching Company offices this afternoon, his friend had expressly told him that his sister was coming to the ball.

Monsale was counting on it. After the passionate embrace the two of them had shared in the Duke of Redditch's town carriage, tonight would be the perfect opportunity to make her jealous. If she saw him sharing sweet words with Lady Euphemia, Naomi might finally realize that the game was over.

And then I will win.

"Do you dance your grace?"

Monsale stirred from his machinations. He had almost forgotten Lady Marshall was standing next to him.

"I don't normally make a habit of it. A bit of a clod on the dance floor. But I can make a turn or two about the room," he replied.

Lady Marshall placed her hand gently on the sleeve of his evening jacket. She nodded in the direction of her daughter and Viscount Walsall. "Euphemia loves to dance; she is quite accomplished."

"And what about her gentleman friend? The viscount seems somewhat taken with her," he replied.

If there was going to have to be an awkward conversation about the obvious attraction between his potential bride and another man, it may as well be now.

Lady Marshall softly sighed. "If you make an offer of marriage to my daughter, rest assured I shall take care of Viscount Walsall. Euphemia will be made to come around. Her being a duchess is far more preferable to ever becoming a viscountess."

Preferable to whom?

He could only wish that Lady Naomi saw things the same way as the countess.

"Well then, I shall be pleased to make your daughter's acquaintance," he replied.

Her maid had barely finished lacing up her gown before Naomi was hurrying out of her bedroom and down the stairs. Reaching the foyer, she came to a sudden halt, and quickly rummaged in her reticule. The final notes on Lady Euphemia Marshall were nowhere to be seen.

"Blast," she whispered.

"Hurry up Naomi. We are already late." Her father

appeared in the front door, motioning to the carriage which stood outside. "Your mother is waiting."

With no time to head back upstairs and collect her papers, Naomi was left scrambling to remember what she had written about lady number three on Monsale's list. Lady Euphemia Marshall.

What did I write?

Pleasant. Good family. Well-bred and socially connected.

I was certain there was something about her that rendered her unsuitable.

Half an hour later, she was still trying to recall the exact details as she followed her parents into the grand house on Silver Street. But the moment she set eyes on Lady Euphemia and Viscount Walsall huddled close to one another, a soft smile came to her lips.

That's it. Euphemia already has an admirer. Her heart is set on the viscount.

Monsale may well be prepared to set his pride aside in order to save his title and lands, but he most certainly wouldn't stand for a wife who might have it in mind to make him a cuckold. Even he had his limits.

Her grin quickly faded the moment Monsale, and Lady Marshall joined them. Instead of giving Viscount Walsall the cold shoulder, Monsale offered him his hand. Lady Euphemia dipped into an elegant curtsy and smiled.

That looks far too friendly and cozy.

She gritted her teeth at the worrying sight. Her jaw clenching tight when polite laughter was exchanged within the gathering.

When a smiling Monsale escorted the earl's daughter out onto the dance floor and slipped his hand about her waist, Naomi feared she might be physically ill.

He has gone too far this time.

She stood rooted to the spot, fighting a rising tide of nausea, as Monsale twirled Lady Euphemia around the floor with effortless grace. So much for his long-held protestations of a lack of dancing skills. The swine.

"He is dancing with her? What the…"

A gentle hand on her arm had Naomi turning from watching what was fast becoming her worst nightmare. Kitty nodded at Monsale and Lady Euphemia. "Don't they make a lovely pair? Monsale looks absolutely smitten."

Naomi glanced back at the dance floor just in time to catch Monsale's eye. He smiled sweetly at her as he and Lady Euphemia swept by.

Traitor.

"He needs to get this marriage business sorted and quick smart. The prince has given him a time and date for the oath ceremony. Eight days from tomorrow, Monsale and his wife have to attend Carlton House."

It took a great deal of effort for Monsale to keep the smile he gifted Naomi to a small one. Given half the chance he would have beamed at her as he twirled by, Lady Euphemia held in his embrace.

See what you are missing dear Naomi.

As soon as his back was to her, he stopped smiling and leaned in to speak to his dance partner.

"When this waltz is over, I would like for you and me to take a stroll out into the garden. Your mother no doubt has explained that there are matters of timely importance for us to discuss."

Lady Euphemia silently nodded. On her face sat a look of heartbreaking despair.

All of Naomi's plans lay in disarray. The sight before her was terrible. As soon as the orchestra had finished playing the waltz, Monsale had taken Lady Euphemia by the arm and led her from the dance floor. They headed through the open doors and disappeared out into the night garden. A man didn't escort a lady to the terrace unless he was serious about her, and his intentions honorable.

This cannot be happening.

She intercepted a passing footman, quickly helping herself to a glass of wine. Before the servant had the chance to walk away, Naomi had downed her drink, then come back for a second. But no amount of alcohol was going to numb her pain.

Somewhere she had made a mistake. A horrid miscalculated, misstep. But where? He couldn't have given up on her after their encounter in the carriage. He must know she had been simply raising the stakes of the bet.

Didn't he?

For the next ten minutes, she stood with her gaze fixed on the French doors. Waiting, praying for Monsale to return. When he finally did, she took heart in the fact that he was alone. But from where she stood, it was difficult to see the expression on his face. He didn't stop to talk to anyone, instead he made his way directly across the floor to where Lady Marshall stood.

They conducted a brief conversation, at the end of which they embraced. A grinning Lady Marshall raced toward the terrace, while a more somber looking Monsale headed for the front door.

What just happened?

Something clearly had been agreed. She could only hazard a guess as to what.

The sickening sensation in her stomach threatened to overwhelm her. Making a quick dash to the ladies retiring room, Naomi found a chair in the farthest corner and dropped into it. She threw her shawl over her head and hid, not caring what anyone else would think if they saw her.

He told me to put my name on the list. I said no. I even slapped him. Oh, dear god, what have I done?

The door of the room opened and was shut firmly. The unmistakable click of a key being turned in the lock echoed in the quiet of the room. Naomi froze.

"I don't want to marry him. I don't love him. I love Walsall."

"Hush now Euphemia. What has love to do with any of this? Monsale is a duke. One of the richest men in all of England. You owe it to your family, and yourself to seal this union."

She caught the sound of skirts shuffling across the room. If she had any sense of decorum, Naomi would make her presence known. But this was the enemy, the woman who was about to steal her man. She sat silent in the chair, listening.

"I don't want to be a duchess. I am quite content to be a viscountess. Walsall is a lovely man; he will make me happy. Monsale is, well…I have heard rumors," replied Euphemia.

Her mother clicked her tongue. "I have it on good authority from Kitty Steele that he is kind and decent where women are concerned. That is all you need to worry about. Give it time, and you won't even remember Viscount Walsall."

A long period of awkward silence followed. Then Euphemia sighed. "No. I will not marry him. I love Simon. Not only that, but I have promised him my heart. You can say what you like Mama, but I am not marrying Monsale."

The key in the door clicked once more, and it was opened.

"You will stay here and think on your words. When you are quite yourself, then you may rejoin the rest of the guests," said Lady Marshall.

"But Mama." Naomi flinched as Lady Marshall closed the door decisively behind her.

"You can't make me marry that brute. He might have all the money in the world, but he will never be my darling Simon," muttered Euphemia.

Following a silent interval, where Naomi could only surmise that Euphemia was quietly sulking, the door finally opened and closed one last time.

I like Lady Euphemia; she has a backbone. She won't be forced into marrying Monsale.

It was now apparent that Monsale had offered for Lady Euphemia. But she in turn, wasn't keen on the match. Unfortunately, the young woman's opinion wasn't the only one which counted. The main issue lay with Lady Marshall. The countess had got her sights set on being the mother-in-law of a duke.

Naomi knew enough from her own experience of being raised in a noble family, that determined society matrons were a force to be reckoned with; and once they had their minds set on something it was nigh on impossible to dissuade them. But if Euphemia continued to stand her ground, she still had a chance.

Is that what I want? He has chosen her—over me. If Euphemia says no, and won't go through with the marriage, Monsale may have to come crawling. But even then, doesn't that make me only the second best? The consolation prize.

After slipping the shawl from her face, Naomi quickly fixed her hair, then headed back into the party. She was badly in need of her mother's counsel.

To her disappointment, the duchess couldn't be found anywhere. The only family member she was able to locate was her father. The Duke of Redditch met her just inside the foyer.

"Ah, there you are, my sweet child. I have been looking everywhere for you. It's not good form that you, an unwed young lady, cannot be easily located at a function. I'll be having a word with your mother regarding this behavior."

I am almost twenty-seven years of age. I am not some naïve debutante.

"Papa, I was in one of the private rooms for the ladies. I promise I wasn't anywhere I shouldn't be, and right this minute I am trying to find Mama. Have you seen her?"

Her father fell silent. An odd expression sat on his face. The duke was by nature a demonstrative man, not one for keeping his thoughts or feelings to himself. Naomi got many of her characteristic traits from him. A quiet Duke of Redditch was usually the portent of something bad.

"She has gone with Monsale. He wished to discuss some private matter with her."

A worried Naomi met his gaze. "What sort of matter?" she pressed.

The duke shook his head. "I think he believes that the list is not working. Or some such thing. The first two candidates for his duchess were from all reports most unsuitable. And while he thinks this third one might do the job admirably; she is apparently unwilling to accept his proposal."

Which leaves me.

There were eight days until Monsale, and his new bride had to swear their oath of fealty before the Prince of Wales. Time was counting down fast.

If Monsale felt the need to urgently speak with the duchess, that could only mean good news. Right this minute, her mother was likely giving her future son-in-law pointers on how he could successfully woo her daughter.

Naomi could almost taste victory. If not tonight, then early tomorrow, Monsale would be on the doorstep of Redditch House requesting a private audience with her father.

How do I play this if he does ask for my hand?

He would have to declare himself. Offer up his heart. Make all the promises he rightly should have made a long time ago. He had kept her waiting all these years, it was only fair that some groveling was involved.

I just want him to say he loves me. It's all I've ever wanted. I can deal with the rest.

She wiped a single tear away, determined to maintain her composure.

"When do you expect Mama to return?"

"I have no idea, but she asked that I take you home. From the sound of things, she and Monsale have much to discuss."

Naomi adjusted her shawl, making ready to step out into the cool of the evening. She could only hope that her mother and Monsale settled their plans quickly. Until Kitty returned home, she wouldn't be able to sleep a wink.

A wedding here in London or at Monsale Castle? The town of Deal, Kent wasn't too far, and she could have her things packed in no time.

That pale green evening gown with the white broderie anglaise on the bodice would be perfect for a wedding dress. Elegant and understated, but still befitting a bride about to become a duchess. I must ask Papa to borrow the family tiara. Or perhaps I should go with the gold gown. Yes, that is a statement piece. Lady Naomi McNeal, Duchess of Monsale.

The gold gown it was.

Naomi gave one last glance around the room, before taking her father's arm. As they headed toward the front door, she caught a glimpse of Lady Marshall and her daughter talking to one another. She couldn't quite catch what they were saying, but the angry look on the countess's face was enough to inform her, that it was a heated conversation.

Well, done, Euphemia, stand up for your heart's desire. I hope you and Viscount Walsall will be happy together.

Now all Naomi had to do was wait for Monsale to pay her a visit and finally concede defeat. Victory was surely hers for the taking.

Chapter Fifteen

E*ight Days to go.*

Naomi was still fully clothed when she woke the following morning. Bright sunlight streamed in the window as she lifted her head from the pillow.

It's morning. I must have fallen asleep.

Rubbing the sleep from her eyes, she sat up, squinting at the elegant French gilded brass and porcelain clock which sat on the mantelpiece. It was well after eight o'clock.

"Why didn't Mama wake me? She must know I would be keen to hear of any news."

She slid quickly off the bed and raced to the mirror. Her hair was somewhat askew from sleep, but at least her attire had survived the night without too many creases. It would have to do. There would be time for changing and having her maid set her wayward tresses once she had spoken to her mother. After that, Naomi expected her morning to be filled with wedding preparations. It was all so very exciting.

Kitty was seated at the table when Naomi stepped into the

dining room. Her mother lifted her gaze from the morning gazette and scowled.

"Did you sleep in your clothes?"

Naomi sheepishly grinned. "Yes. I was waiting for you to arrive home. Papa said you and Monsale were having urgent discussions. Would that conversation happen to be about me?"

With a wave of her hand, the duchess dismissed the pair of footmen, standing to attention on the other side of the table. As soon as they had left the room, she pulled out the chair next to hers and patted its cushion. "Come and sit here. You and I need to talk."

Taking a seat Naomi confidently adjusted her skirts. This was a red-letter day. A day which she had been waiting for, for a very long time.

Kitty folded the newspaper and sat with her hands resting gently in her lap. "You are correct in your thinking that Monsale and I had a long conversation last night. He was most concerned that Lady Euphemia Marshall, lady number three, might refuse his suit."

Naomi nervously straightened her back. "I see."

"And he was correct."

A sigh of relief escaped Naomi's lips. "Oh, thank god for that," she muttered.

"But..."

She froze, not liking that word.

"Monsale spoke to Lady Euphemia in the garden and addressed her concerns. She was still uncertain, but then Lady Marshall, and Monsale talked to her once more. Euphemia finally came to see sense and has agreed to marry Monsale. His lands and title will now be safe. He asked that I extend to you his kind regards and deepest gratitude for your efforts with his selection of a bride."

It took some time for Naomi's brain to process her mother's words. They kept getting jumbled up and tripping over one another. Eventually, she was able to put them into some semblance of order. Monsale. Bride. Euphemia.

He had chosen Lady Euphemia to be his wife.

"Naomi?"

"When is the wedding?" she asked in a voice barely above a whisper.

"They are to be married at Monsale Castle in three days. Monsale would have pushed for an earlier date, but Lady Marshall insisted on having time to get her daughter's trousseau put together. It will be a small affair, but I am pleased to say that we have all been invited," replied Kitty.

Naomi had heard mention of people claiming they had been struck numb with shock, but she hadn't ever thought such a thing could happen to her. Her whole body had lost all sense of feeling. It was a wonder she was still able to breathe.

When Kitty lay a hand over hers, she didn't feel it. Her eyes tracked the movement, but it seemed like watching a play from a distance. None of it was real.

"Are you alright Naomi?"

"I...I don't know."

The odd sensation of numbness disappeared as a wave of despair crashed over her. Monsale was getting married. To another woman. Those words rolled over and over in her mind.

And then the tears came, floods of them. All her hopes and dreams were crushed to dust.

"Oh, you silly girl. What have you done?" whispered Kitty.

She pushed away her mother's attempt to console her and got to her feet. Desperate sobs of heartache echoed in the quiet space. "Monsale. No."

"You didn't want to be on the list. Naomi, you left him with no other choice. His families fortune and the Monsale title were in peril, he had to choose one of them."

"No. No, he didn't. He could have finally accepted that he

and I were meant to be together. That our love was worth taking the risk. But he was a bloody coward. I can't believe he would condemn himself to a loveless union rather than open his heart to me."

Naomi wrapped her arms about herself, hugging tight. This had always been a game of chance, and the stakes set high. She had thought she knew which way the dice were going to land. Certain that they were loaded in her favor, Naomi had gambled everything.

And lost.

Chapter Sixteen

E*ight Days to go.*

With his wedding only a matter of days away, Monsale had to avail himself of a special license from the Archbishop of Canterbury. An expensive privilege offered to only a few such as the nobility.

On his way home from Doctors' Common, Monsale stopped by the home of George and Jane Hawkins in Coal Yard Lane. The pregnant Jane and her rounded baby belly greeted him at the door.

"Your grace, what a lovely surprise. Come in."

As he stepped through the front door into the cozy, old home, Jane called upstairs to her husband. "George, Monsale is here."

The thud of heavy boots on the narrow, oak stairs announced the arrival of the Honorable George Hawkins. "Good morning. You are up and about early. It's just past eleven."

Monsale ignored the remark about his habit of being a late

riser. He had never been an early bird. Late the previous night he had sent word to his friends of his impending marriage and an invitation to the wedding at Monsale Castle.

"Lots to do before the wedding. I had assumed that a chap just turned up and stood in front of the minister, said yes a few times, and that was it," he replied.

He accepted a congratulatory kiss on the cheek from Jane. "I hope you will be very happy."

They followed her down the hallway and into the kitchen which was situated at the rear of the house. The house overlooked a small, well-tended plot of land filled with vegetables and raised herb beds. Monsale's gaze roamed appreciatively over the garden as he pulled out a chair and sat.

"I must bring you some of my rose bushes to plant along the border. Make things look pretty."

Jane and George exchanged a look of surprise. Monsale simply chuckled. "I am about to become a married man; I need to be able to talk about these things."

"May I offer you a cup of tea or a slice of cake?" asked Jane.

"I think that would possibly be a bridge too far for the impending bachelor, my love. I think a whisky might be more welcome," said George.

He kissed his wife and spoke quietly to her before Jane left the kitchen. The click of the front door closing soon followed.

"I didn't mean to drive her out of the house," said Monsale.

"You have always had a strange effect on women. But fear not, Jane has an appointment at Captain and Mrs. Jones house. Gus's mother is hosting a luncheon for Evangeline. Apparently, she has taken quite a shine to her new daughter-in-law and is doing everything to make her feel welcome."

It was a relief to hear that Mrs. Jones had forgiven the French-born Evangeline for having stolen her youngest son away to go and live in Brittany. "Gus says they are already planning to have his parents come to stay at Château-de-La-Roche. Captain Jones is interested in the work they are putting into the new roof beams that are being installed in the east wing of the main house."

Repairs to the fire damaged château were going to take a long time. It was a pity Monsale wouldn't ever be able to see them. France was the one country he would never dare to try to visit again. There were still several outstanding warrants for his arrest. The French navy wasn't likely to ever forgive the man who had stolen three of their ships.

George took a seat in a chair on the opposite side of the table from where Monsale sat. He produced a whisky flask from his jacket pocket and offered it to him. Monsale shook his head. "No, I have too many things to do this afternoon."

His friend narrowed his eyes. "Are you well?"

"Yes. Just a little…" he sighed.

"A little what?"

The words stuck in his mouth. It was hard enough to accept that he was nervous, saying it was nigh on impossible.

"I'm a little unsure of myself. Marriage is a huge step."

Especially when it likely included him having to make the sacrifice that the rest of the rogues of the road had all done as they took on wives. Giving up the darker side of the business. Setting aside illegal work and doing his best to become an honest man was going to take some doing.

Monsale had wrestled with the problem for the past year, long before the Prince of Wales had thrown the fealty oath into the mix. If he was going to ever be a father who his children could look up to, he had to move on from a life of crime.

"How did you do it?" he asked.

A look of realization appeared on George's face. "You are not worried about getting married, it's the other thing that concerns you. Walking away from the old life? Ah, yes, my friend, I can understand exactly how you are feeling right now. I must be honest with you, its bloody scary. For a time, I wasn't sure I could do it."

"But you did."

"Yes. Love makes you reassess everything. When it came down to a choice between having Jane in my life or staying a thief, the decision was surprisingly easy. I'm just not sure how you will deal with it."

George left the rest of the obvious unsaid. He had given up his life of crime for a woman he loved. Monsale was getting married because he had to save his family fortune. Love wasn't playing a part in it.

"I've been under no illusion that it would take time to untangle myself from the web of dubious business deals I've been mixed up in, but over the past year, I have been slowly pulling back from them. The only major outstanding piece is the smuggling operation, and that's more down to Gus's reluctance to give it up," replied Monsale.

The McNeal family hadn't always been criminals. Before the death of his wife, James McNeal, had been a good man who only dabbled in the odd bit of government sanctioned privateering. Grief had seen him throw his respectable life away and become a full-blown pirate, taking Andrew with him.

George took a sip from the whisky flask, then stuffed it back into his jacket.

"If you have been withdrawing from the life over the past year, you must have had in mind to marry sometime soon. Which means, knowing you your grace, that a particular woman must have been on your mind. And I don't mean Lady Euphemia Marshall."

He held out his hand, and George quickly passed him the flask. Flipping it open, Monsale took a long drink.

"I gave Naomi every chance to put her name on the list. She repeatedly refused. A man can only take no for an answer, so many times."

George winced. He and Jane were good friends of Naomi, which made this whole thing painfully awkward.

"I just wonder if perhaps you didn't give her a chance. Jane doesn't think you treated her very well. Says you shouldn't have ever put Naomi in the position where she had to compete to become your duchess."

Thank you, Jane, I could have done with your sage advice earlier.

"It's done. So just leave it alone. Besides, the last time Naomi and I spoke, she told me she hated me."

He wasn't going to make mention that he had been kissing Naomi and trying to grope her breast at the time. Or that she had struck him with some force.

The look on her face before she had slapped his face, had kept Monsale awake the previous night. He should have been staring at the ceiling worrying about his impending marriage, but instead all he could think of was Naomi's soft sighs and the overwhelming sense that she would have given him everything there and then if only he had said those three little words.

"Be my duchess."

Tell yourself all the lies you want. They are not the words she needs to hear first from your lips. She wants to hear the other three little words.

Chapter Seventeen

After leaving Coal Yard Lane, Monsale instructed his driver to head to Gracechurch Street and the rear mews of the RR Coaching Company. Once he had alighted, his carriage turned around and headed back to Monsale House. He liked to keep his household staff away from the rogues of the road dealings, and always took a hack home once he had finished with company business.

The stable hand Bob appeared from out of a nearby building, trailed by his three-legged dog, Snick. Monsale gave him a wave in greeting, to which Bob gave a nod. "Morning your grace. Will you be upstairs or elsewhere in the yard?"

"Good morning, Bob. It will be the stables today. I need to make a withdrawal."

Monsale bent and gave the old bulldog, Snick, a friendly scratch behind the ear. The dog actually belonged to Stephen's younger brother Toby, but every time they had moved it to the house on Berkeley Square, Snick had managed to find his way back to the coaching company.

Scraggy old Bob cleared his throat. "I was going to ask how my investments are going this quarter. I've been reading the financial pages and there are some new mines I was thinking I might like to put some money into."

Monsale shook his head. "You are getting a good and safe return from Coutts Bank at present. I would caution you to steer clear of unproven mines and get-rich-quick schemes. We need to preserve your money, so you can retire to a life of leisure and fresh air in the countryside. There is a new investment opportunity coming very soon, one which will give a reliable flow of cash in the years to come. I have your name on the list of initial investors."

Bob bowed. "Very good your grace. Thank you. If you are going to the stables, I shall get my rifle and stand guard."

"Capital. Remember to signal if anyone arrives in the yard."

While the stable hand went to retrieve his weapon, Monsale headed to the back of the stables. Kicking away the thick covering of straw, he uncovered a trapdoor. It took both hands to pull the door up and flip it open. It landed with a thud on the brick paved floor. Taking care, Monsale slowly descended the stone steps which led down to a secret underground room. As he entered the small space, all noise from the world above disappeared. It was almost like stepping into a crypt, but one without any sarcophagi.

There was a huge iron door, situated against one wall, it was locked and bolted. Monsale smiled. It had been his idea to build the room and install the safe. The large padlock on the front, which was a false lock, had been George's clever innovation.

Fishing into his coat pocket, he took out a small key, then slipped it into a tiny, almost invisible, keyhole which sat to one side of the main lock. A satisfying click came from within the safe. Monsale pulled on the handle and the iron door swung silently open. Reformed thief, George had always been fastidious about ensuring that the hinges and locks were regularly oiled.

On the bottom shelf of the safe sat a large box, marked A.M. At one point there had been five of these boxes, one for each member of the RR Coaching Company. They had dubbed them their flee boxes, the jest being that there was enough money and treasure in them to enable anyone of the rogues of the road to flee England should the authorities uncover their illegal activities.

As each member of the company had married and retired from the life, they had taken their box with them. Now only Monsale's remained.

He sat the box on the floor and stared at it. Once this box had been a source of comfort, the means to safely start a new life somewhere else, now it only served to remind him of the dark and often dangerous times he and his friends had been fortunate to survive.

Bending, he set another key to the box and unlocked it. Inside were rare jewels, gold, share certificates, and several large bundles of banknotes. He ignored them. Instead, he lifted a small blue cotton bag, untied the string around the top of it and dropped yet another key into the palm of his hand.

Back at the safe, Monsale squeezed into the space between it and the side wall. After fitting the key into a hidden lock, he pulled another box out. This one was long and narrow, but what it lacked in size it more than made up for with what it contained.

Inside were records of bank deposits and various other documents. It was his secret hoard. No other member of the RR Coaching Company even knew it existed. Adan was the only person he trusted with the knowledge of the box.

Monsale sighed. It was time to retire both it and the flee box. He would sleep better knowing that the hidden space under the stables was finally empty.

The scruff of boots above his head had Monsale quickly digging his hand into his coat pocket. He pulled out his pistol, cocked it, and with a steady hand pointed it at the steps.

"Don't shoot," said a familiar voice.

Gus appeared; hands held high above his head.

"Bloody hell. What are you doing here? And why didn't Bob let out a warning whistle."

So much for the old man keeping watch in the yard. And not even the dog had a noise.

Maybe it is time to retire Bob and Snick from the job.

Gus's gaze fell on the secret box. "Dare I ask what that is?"

Monsale put the weapon away. "It's the wealth I have been building from all our business endeavors. A piece of extra insurance. I figured that if the time ever came that one of us had to flee the country, the rest would soon have to follow. This fortune would allow Adan to smooth the way without anyone knowing the money was ours."

Gus nodded. The expression on his face was one of guarded acceptance. Considering the shady dealings that Monsale had conducted over the years; Gus's reaction didn't surprise him in the least. He had kept his friends in the dark about this box and its priceless contents.

"I saw George earlier, he told me you are planning on giving up the criminal trade. Following him, Harry, and Stephen, into an honest life. I came to ask you where that leaves Evangeline and me?" said Gus.

Monsale closed up both boxes and cradled them in his arms. "Come up to the company offices and let's talk."

He had never been comfortable spending more time than necessary in the room under the stables. His greatest fear had always been that someone would happen to discover its existence and decided to conduct a raid while he was inside. If they did, he wouldn't stand a chance. He was far too young to be left for dead in a hole in the ground.

Upstairs in the office, Monsale and Gus each took a seat at

the big, old, weather-beaten table. Monsale gently set the boxes down.

Gus stared at his hands for a moment, then cleared his throat. "I think we should seriously consider closing up the smuggling operation. These days I am spending a good deal of my time on the rebuilding of the château, and the new men living on the estate are busy planting crops. The former members of the Lamballe smuggling gang are keen to forge new lives as farmers. Evangeline and I have talked about investing more of our money in developing the land."

Monsale could understand where his friend's mind was at, and also his heart. He wanted the same. A life without constantly looking over his shoulder, of wondering if and when it might all come to a sudden end.

"When the Prince of Wales started being friendly to me at the cookbook launch, the first thing I thought was that they were coming for me. Adan had my yacht moved to Dover, and our contingency plans were ready to be put into action," replied Monsale.

Through his sources at Carlton House, he knew that the prince regent was still sore over not getting his hands on the treasure which George and Jane had uncovered a few months earlier. The court had ruled that they had the right of finders keeper and had thrown out the royal claim. Monsale's initial thoughts had been that the prince was looking for revenge.

Tapping his finger on the top of the flee box, he met Gus's eye. "I don't want to live like that anymore either, I've had a lifetime of thievery, blood, and danger. I need to get out. And so do you and your new bride. That's why the RR Coaching Company will be holding an extraordinary meeting before you and Evangeline leave at the end of next week."

Monsale's long-held plans would finally be revealed.

Gus frowned. "Won't you be on your honeymoon?"

"The honeymoon will have to wait. The oath needs to be

made before the prince on the twenty-fourth. Only after my fortunes have been secured will I even think about the post wedding arrangements."

"I am sorry that this whole business with Prinny has meant that you are being forced into a marriage with someone you barely know. To be honest, I don't think I could do it. I just hope that in time the two of you can find a way to live together. To create a comfortable existence where you can raise a family."

Monsale closed up the box and got to his feet. The next few days were going to be difficult.

"Lady Euphemia seems a nice enough girl. We should all give her a chance," he replied.

Gus said nothing, but it was clear he wanted to say more. Monsale had a horrible suspicion it had a great deal to do with Lady Naomi Steele.

"What else do you have to do before the wedding?" asked Gus.

"A few more minor things. I'm leaving for Monsale Castle this afternoon. Adan will be accompanying me. It's only right and proper that everything be perfectly arranged for the arrival of the new Duchess of Monsale."

If everyone was going to have to make the best of a bad situation then it should be done in comfort and splendor.

If he was any sort of honorable bridegroom, he would be sending gifts to his intended, paying her attention before the wedding. But he wasn't. His agreement with Euphemia was based purely on business and the protection of his family's future.

Euphemia deserved more than he could ever give her.

She deserves to be with someone she loves. And who loves her.

He headed for the door. "I will see you at my buck's turn."

And while the wine and whisky stocks of Monsale Castle were sure to take a hammering the night before the wedding, he was certain that in the morning there was going to be more than one painful headache for which he was going to have to find a cure.

Chapter Eighteen

Being forced to attend the wedding of the man she had always thought she would marry, while he took another woman as his wife, was a particular form of cruelty in Naomi's opinion. She had offered to remain in London, and avoid the trip to Deal, but Kitty wouldn't hear of it.

"You played the game and lost. Now you have to face up to the consequences. I'm sorry if this wedding is going to be difficult for you my dear, but you only have yourself to blame."

Her mother's words were cold, but true. Somewhere she had made a grave mistake; she had assumed Monsale felt more for her than he actually did.

Standing hands on hips paying the barest of attention while her maid packed her travel trunk, Naomi considered the developments of the past week.

Where did I go wrong? He wanted my name on the list. He kissed me.

After an afternoon of shopping earlier in the day, she had called in at Monsale House, bearing a small congratulatory gift for the betrothed couple. In truth her intentions had been to talk to Monsale, to confront him.

To try to change—anything. Everything.

The footman who answered the door had explained that the duke had left for Kent late the previous day. He assured her that he would make certain that the generous gift eventually found its way to the happy couple. Naomi was left with no other option than to leave the present and go.

Crushed, she had promptly returned home. All the years of loving and wanting Monsale's heart had come to naught.

Chapter Nineteen

The Wedding Eve
Monsale Castle
The Kentish Coast

The wedding guests all arrived over the course of the afternoon. To Monsale's relief the Marshalls arrived last. The bride and her parents immediately headed up to the main guest chambers where they remained sequestered and out of sight from everyone.

When supper time came, Lady Marshall sent word that Euphemia was feeling poorly and would be taking her meal in the privacy of her room. Pre-wedding jitters were to be expected.

Another groom might see that as a portent of bad things to come, but Monsale was more than happy to spend his last night as a bachelor in the company of his friends. Tomorrow was going to be hard enough.

He offered the earl and countess the use of one of the castle's smaller dining rooms and they, along with the Duke and Duchess of Redditch dined separately from the rest of the wedding guests. With Lady Euphemia Marshall slated to be the Duchess of Monsale in a matter of hours, her mother was more than happy to be accorded the respect of her future role of mother-in-law.

The grand hall of the castle was being prepared for the wedding, so Monsale hosted the rest of his guests in another room which overlooked the sea.

As he stepped into the room, he stopped to take in the sight. A roaring fire burned brightly in the fireplace. It made the room toasty and inviting. He was tempted to remove his coat but kept it on. After this meal, he had other matters to attend to in the castle grounds.

The table was set with all manner of supper delights. He had wisely instructed Adan to bring the Monsale House chef with him in the servants coach. From the look of the sliced ham, elegantly stuffed mushrooms, and plates of small chicken pies he deduced he had been forgiven for the disaster of the evening with the Shadbolt family.

Around the table, were seated all his nearest and dearest friends. Gus and Evangeline. George and Jane. Stephen and Bridget. Lady Alice.

He scowled. Where were Harry and Naomi? His inquiring gaze met that of Alice, and she pointed back over his shoulder. He turned as Harry placed a firm hand on his shoulder.

"Sorry I am late. Could I have a word?"

They stepped out of the room and Monsale ushered his friend into a nearby sitting room, closing the door behind him. "What's wrong?" he asked.

"Naomi won't be joining us for supper. She has cried off with a headache. In fact, you should know that she is not at the castle. It took quite some effort to get her into the travel coach, and she only finally agreed to come if she could stay somewhere else," replied Harry.

"So where is she?"

This wasn't good news. He needed Naomi at the castle.

"My father spoke to your man Adan, and he put my sister up in one of the estate cottages further along the beach. She has her maid and a castle footman with her, so she is perfectly safe."

Monsale sighed. Naomi's current position was completely understandable. She had likely thought that this would be the night before her wedding. Not that she was going to be merely a guest. Her nonappearance, however, was not in Monsale's plans. It had him worried.

I have to see her.

He had to know whether she was simply hiding away, stewing in anger, or if she was avoiding him in order to hide her tears. Neither answer sat well with him.

I've hurt her. I know it.

"Can I ask you to do something for me? A favor that will mean I am forever in your debt," he said.

Harry blinked slowly. Asking favors of his friends was a given when it came to Monsale but repaying them was unheard of. In fact, it bordered on mythical.

"What do you need from me?"

"I need you to make sure that Naomi is here at the castle first thing tomorrow. Things are happening which I cannot currently discuss with anyone, but rest assured everything will become clear in the morning. What I can tell you, is that a great deal of my future rests on your sister being here. Just make sure she doesn't get cold feet and decide to take the family coach back to London at first light."

Harry gave him a look which said that he was deeply suspicious of Monsale's motives. "You ask a great deal of me my friend. My sister is broken-hearted over you. Her pride is all that she has left, and I can tell you that she doesn't have much of it in abundance."

He would dearly love to tell Harry the truth. Of how Naomi had played the game as strongly as he had, but the way ahead was not yet clear.

The problem of Lady Euphemia Marshall, his fiancée, still had to be addressed.

He met Harry's gaze. "Would it make you feel any better to know that I too have suffered? I made a mistake with the list and have paid dearly for it. But I swear I never set out to hurt Naomi."

Harry nodded. "I shall do what I can. But don't be surprised if she doesn't stay long after the wedding service. I, for one, won't make Naomi remain at the castle a minute longer than is necessary. If she is in pieces after you marry Euphemia, I am going to bundle her, Alice, and my sweet little boy into my coach and promptly take them all home."

Monsale nodded. If things went according to plan, Naomi would be more than happy to remain at the castle after the wedding.

A knock came at the door, and Adan poked his head inside.

"Your grace, they are making a run for it."

A smile crept to Monsale's lips. "Thank you. Excuse me Harry, I have some urgent business to attend to in the stables. I'll join the rest of the supper gathering as soon as I can."

Harry narrowed his eyes. "For your sake, I hope that means what I think it does."

Monsale stepped toward the door, stopped on the threshold, and glanced back at his friend.

"So do I."

Buttoning up his coat, he headed for the stairs. Every step down to the ground floor was in time with his hard-thumping heart. Everything, his entire future, would be dictated by the events of the next few minutes.

Chapter Twenty

The wind whistled through the trees. A leaf crushed under Monsale's boot as he made his way across the dark courtyard toward the stables.

He could just imagine seeing the fabled Sir Gawain's headless Green Knight ride out of the nearby woods. Or even a ghost if he was particularly lucky. But Monsale had experienced enough mayhem in his life to know that the stories couldn't match reality.

Fortunately, his quarry this evening was alive and if the volume of supposed whispering was any indication, very much in possession of their heads.

I would never ask either of you to undertake a mission involving stealth. Talk about making a commotion.

Reaching the stables, he slipped in through the side entrance. The sight which met his eyes in the dim light had Monsale chuckling into the sleeve of his coat.

Viscount Walsall was attempting, and failing, to get Euphemia onto the back of a horse. Every time she managed to get her foot in the stirrups, the animal shifted, and she was forced to hop after it. Walsall was holding on to the back of

Euphemia's gown trying to pull her away. If the situation wasn't so perilous for them all, Monsale would have laughed.

"If you are going to steal one of my horses, I would suggest you might want to pick a less frisky one. Sinbad is known for his dislike of females."

Walsall and Euphemia both froze as Monsale sauntered out from his hiding place and into the light. The earl clearly hadn't planned the moonlight flit all that well.

He immediately let go of Euphemia and with his fists raised, marched toward Monsale. Grim determination sat on his countenance.

Excellent. I do like a chap who is prepared to fight for what he wants.

"Euphemia is mine. She and I are leaving this evening. If you try to stop us, I swear I shall do you grave harm," said Walsall.

Monsale punched the air. "Now that is the sort of spirit I like in a man. Knows what he wants and is determined to take it. But calm yourself Walsall, I haven't changed my mind, nor am I about to renege on the deal Lady Euphemia and I made at the ball. You are still eloping tonight."

He turned to Euphemia. "I don't think going by horseback is going to work. The last thing any of us wish is for the two of you to come to grief out on the road."

Walsall speared his fingers through his tussled hair. "I was planning on taking my coach, but I had to hide it out on the road a mile or so back. Couldn't risk anyone seeing it."

"Papa asked our driver to sleep in the coach and keep an eye out for anyone who tries to leave, so we couldn't take the Marshall one. My parents won't rest until I am the Duchess of Monsale," said Euphemia.

Of course, they won't. The countess is determined to make her daughter a duchess whether she likes it or not.

He nodded at the horse. "That beast is not going to get you very far. He has a frightful temper and will do everything he can to throw a shoe. You will be walking the best part of the night with him. Walsall, take my travel coach. I'll give you the use of some of my stable staff and a driver to take you to your coach. Make for Lower Eythorne tonight, I own a small cottage in the village, so you can stay there. It's eleven miles from here, far enough to give you a good head start in the morning for Scotland."

Walsall and Euphemia exchanged hopefully glances. "What about you?" asked Walsall.

Monsale held out his hand, and the two men shook. "When Euphemia's absence is discovered in the morning, I will play the role of surprised, and disappointed bridegroom. I shall of course garner sympathy and admiration by being the picture of stoic English male. By the time everyone understands the truth of what has happened, the two of you will be well on your way to the border."

A tearful Euphemia rushed forward and placed a kiss on his cheek. "Thank you. We are so deeply grateful. One day, you shall make a wonderful husband to some lucky woman."

I sincerely hope that is the case. And that it's tomorrow.

"May you both be blessed with a long and happy life together. Euphemia, I shall head back inside and organize to have the rest of your things collected and put in my coach. Stay here out of sight, we can't risk your mother deciding to come and have a pre-wedding night chat," said Monsale.

He left the stables, satisfied that for once in his life he had done a noble, selfless thing. But he knew that ridding himself of his fiancée was the easy part, now he had to find a way to get Naomi to stop being angry with him. To finally put an end to their stubborn battle of wills.

Making his way up the stairs a short while later, he steered clear of the guest bedrooms. The less noise there was in the castle living quarters the better. The last thing he needed was to accidentally meet up with either of Naomi or Euphemia's parents.

Stuffing his hands into the deep pockets of his coat, Monsale headed out through a nearby doorway. It led to the long set of steps which ran all the way down the side of the castle to the grassy lawn far below. It was a short walk across the outer bailey, over the low sand dunes, after which he finally made it to the beach.

Between now and the scheduled time for the wedding he had to find Naomi and get her to agree to marry him.

Easier said than done.

She had avoided the guided tour of the castle which Adan had hosted. And her absence at supper would have been noted by now.

There wasn't much he could do about the situation. He would just have to trust Harry to come up with a plausible story which explained Naomi's absence.

I'm sure they all know how things are between Naomi and myself, so her not being at the supper won't need much explanation.

And as long as the Marshalls and Steeles all remained tucked up enjoying a splendid supper, along with the castle's best French brandy and wine, all that was left for him to do was to continue with the pretense of intending to make Lady Euphemia his wife tomorrow morning. That task should be nothing more than a trifling deception for Monsale, he was used to lies.

I just wish this tight knot in my stomach would go away.

The spicy scent of a burning cigar reached his nose, he looked back over his shoulder to see Harry standing a few yards away. There was a pensive look on his friend's face.

"You didn't come back in for supper. Standing on the beach seems a strange way to celebrate your last night of freedom," said Harry.

"I wasn't hungry."

Harry moved closer and offered Monsale the cigar. He took it and inhaled a long drag before blowing the pale gray smoke out into the night, where the sea breeze caught it and whipped it away.

"I saw something peculiar a short time ago. Your travel coach was headed out the main driveway. And I could have sworn that Lady Euphemia Marshall was on board," said Harry.

Monsale focused his gaze on the whitecaps of the waves as they slowly rolled their way to the shore.

"Really? Perhaps she left something behind in London and had to nip back home to retrieve it."

Harry snorted. "It's nigh on seventy miles to town. It would want to be the crown jewels if she is going to attempt such a journey in the dark. What's going on?"

Monsale handed the cigar back to his friend. "Things are not what they seem. Suffice to say, Lady Euphemia and I shall not be getting married in the morning. She and Viscount Walsall are headed for Scotland."

Do I risk telling him the truth? Swear him to secrecy until the morning.

"Does that explain your pressing need for Naomi to be at the castle in the morning? If it does, what else can I do to help?"

Until now, his plans had been kept a closely guarded secret between himself and Adan. Harry was Naomi's brother, he really ought to be trusted when it came to aiding her future happiness.

"What would you say if I told you, I have been a complete ass? And I don't mean just a small one. I have made an unholy mess of things with your sister. Tomorrow morning, I intend to rectify that situation."

"Ah, so that is why you are out here staring into the dark sea. Looking for nature's inspiration as to how you can convince Naomi to become your duchess. An interesting strategy, though not how I would have approached things," replied Harry.

Monsale shook his head. Harry was going to make him beg for his help.

And rightly so. He loves Naomi. And is going to punish me on her behalf. I would do the same if she were my sister.

"Harry, dear old chap. Friend of all friends. Pray tell me what the devil I am going to do? I have to find a way to get Naomi to forgive me, then agree to be my wife. When it comes to women, I am prepared to admit to being uneven on my feet. And with Naomi, I have always been walking on wet sand."

Monsale winced as Harry clapped his hands together. He could also have done without the long deep laugh.

"Monsale. Monsale. Monsale. What can I say?"

I am beginning to think you shutting up might be a better option.

They moved away from the water and headed further along the beach. If anyone happened to come out from the castle grounds, they wouldn't be able to see them walking along the sand.

"Let me ask you this, do you love my sister? I know you need to save your title and lands, but I am still not prepared to offer my assistance if all Naomi is going to get in return for marrying you is an empty union. Not even for you would I sacrifice her happiness."

"Yes Harry, I do love Naomi. And the more I think about it, I accept that I have probably been in love with her for many years."

There was a hard lump in his throat at finally giving voice to that emotion. His greatest fear now was that just as he had come to accept his feelings for Naomi, he might very well be on the verge of losing her forever.

I do. I love her. And I am not going to let her go.

"Well then, you need to go to her. Confess your feelings. Offer her marriage. Finally, allow Naomi to put all this god-awful heartbreak behind her. She has endured years of pain because of you. And I must confess there were times when I have hated you for it."

Monsale frowned at Harry. "Have I really made it that hard for her?" He knew the answer to that question. Of course, he had. A man would have to be willfully blind not to have seen the look of disappointment on Naomi's face every time he refused to dance with her.

"You aren't honestly going to stand there and tell me that you didn't know she has been in love with you forever? Everyone else has been able to see it, why not you," said Harry.

"No, I wouldn't do either of you that sort of disservice. Naomi's love was something I turned away from all those years because I didn't think I would be good enough for her. I am not an honest man, I'm a liar, and a thief at best, at worst—well you know the rest. This list of potential brides has been a complete disaster, and it's all my fault. I thought it would be an easy way to get her to put her hand up, and for me to select Naomi as my wife without having to finally admit how I felt. But all I have managed to do is to break her heart."

Monsale rubbed his hands over the tension spots on his forehead. He was waiting for Harry to give him a well-deserved piece of his mind. To confirm that, he was indeed a bloody fool. And that Naomi shouldn't marry him.

"Do you honestly think that this love lark has been easy on any of us? I almost lost Alice. Jane shot George. Bridget threw Stephen out. And from what I hear, Gus didn't have a smooth ride when it came to Evangeline. But what we have all done, is not given up. And you have to do the same."

He desperately wanted to go to Naomi tonight, but he owed it to Euphemia and Walsall to stay silent. To give them the best chance of making it to Scotland before Lord and Lady Marshall discovered the truth of their daughter's disappearance.

"It will have to wait until morning before I speak to Naomi. If the Marshall's get wind of what has just happened, there will be all hell to pay."

"Well then may I suggest you get rid of Lord and Lady Marshall as soon as you can tomorrow morning. Spare their daughter from the wrath of her parents by telling them it was you who called off the wedding. That should get them angry enough to leave posthaste."

Monsale liked that idea.

That would then clear the way for him to seek Naomi out and try to salvage their relationship.

Walsall had come for Euphemia. Shown her the strength of his love. Now it was his turn. He had to do something grand for Naomi.

"It's no good me simply telling Naomi that she has always been the one. I have to show her. Make her finally see, that she has my heart."

Harry held his hands to the heavens and cheered. "Hallelujah, the message has finally gotten through. Monsale, for a smart man, you can be incredibly dull witted, especially when it comes to women and love."

Monsale snatched the cigar out of his friend's fingers and drew back on it deeply. Tomorrow he would deal with the Marshalls, then he would make Naomi his wife.

But first he had to convince her that he was worth the risk.

"I need Naomi out here in the morning no later than eight o'clock?

Harry was silent for a time. It was to be expected. He was fiercely protective of his sister. Seeing her in pain over her love for Monsale must surely be giving him cause for concern. Marriage wasn't just a trivial thing such as a missed dance.

"I will bring Naomi here, but I won't make her stay. Who knows what the past few days have done to alter the way she feels about you. Promise me that you will not hold it against her if she says the damage is too great."

Monsale took another long puff of the cigar. "Just make sure you bring her to the beach in the morning. I will take care of the rest."

He handed Harry the cigar and turned to head back to the castle. His friends would have to forgive his non-appearance at supper tonight.

Andrew McNeal, Duke of Monsale, had grand gestures of love to plan.

Chapter Twenty-One

Regret sat bitter in Naomi's mouth as she stepped out onto the expanse of the beach the following morning. She normally loved the sea; the cries of the seagulls as they soared high overhead were a siren's call to her soul.

But not this morning, even the blue skies and refreshing salt air could not bring her a sense of serenity. She would rather be anywhere but here at Monsale Castle. Her protests and offer to remain in London had been refused by her mother. She had made her bed and was now going to have to lie in it.

The thought of standing amongst the guests watching while Monsale made Lady Euphemia his duchess had bile rising in her throat. She was certain there were no more tears left to cry.

How am I going to get through today without falling to pieces?

Her stomach was empty, she couldn't face food this morning. If she were honest about it, there were few things she could stand right now. Being alone offered the only glint of solace for her broken heart.

Naomi glanced over at her brother; Harry walked alongside her. She hadn't even been granted the peace of being left alone. Instead, he had been at the door of the cottage a little after seven, rousing her from her bed with the unexpected offer of a long walk on the beach.

She knew what he was doing. Keeping her busy before the wedding ceremony at ten o'clock. Stopping her from leaving.

Why do I have to attend? He is your friend. Can't people just let me keep one small piece of my self-regard intact?

Wet sand crunched under her boots as they made their way along the beach toward the castle. The towering ancient fortress of Monsale Castle dominated the landscape. She couldn't escape it. It was a constant reminder of her failure. Of the game she had played and lost.

In a matter of hours Monsale would be walking down the aisle and taking another woman as his bride. By the time the sun had set on this day he would belong to someone else.

Euphemia would be the one to share his bed. To give birth to his children. To see him through the years ahead and be by his side as he grew old. And as a family friend, she would be forced to bear witness to it all. To endure every painful celebration of the Duke and Duchess of Monsale's lives. Constantly reminded of what she had gambled and lost.

A tear snaked down her cheek. How many tears had she already shed over the past few days?

Why isn't there a limit on the number of times you can cry over someone?

She stared out to sea, the coast of France a thin dark line in the distance. Travel beckoned. The Steele family had land holdings in Ireland, perhaps when this day was over, she would speak to her parents and suggest she leave England for a time. The fresh air and green vista of another land might help to heal her heart. Allow her time to begin to pick up the pieces, and perhaps find hope once more.

Her gaze drifted to the nearby holm of Saint Margaret which lay a short distance across the water. On the top of a small rise stood the ruins of a medieval monastic church. She had always wanted to visit the tiny island. Had held secret dreams of hosting summer picnics on the grassy knoll next to the chapel.

But that had been when she saw her future as Monsale's duchess. That dream was now at an end.

"I just wish Mama wasn't so insistent on me attending the service," she muttered.

She could well understand her mother's reasons. Refusing to take part in the celebrations would be hypocritical in the least. It had been her decision not to put her name on the list. Monsale had asked more than once. A man could only take no for an answer so many times before he looked elsewhere for a wife.

"You know why you have to go to the wedding. Mama and Papa consider Monsale to be a part of the family. It would be an insult not to make an appearance," replied Harry.

As opposed to the groom marrying another woman after he had kissed me and begged me to put my name on his list?

She would take that humiliating experience with her to the grave.

With a resigned sigh, Naomi continued on toward the castle. The rest of the shoreline behind them was ragged rocks and inaccessible drops to the sea. The only other place to walk was inland and into the nearby village of Deal.

A figure appeared at the crest of one of the dunes leading down from the castle. From the way they were dressed it was obviously a man. Naomi peered, straining to see if it was another of her brother's friends. Whoever it was, they were headed her way.

Damn. The last thing I want to do this morning is make polite conversation.

She turned on her heel and slowly began to walk back the way they had come. Hopefully, whoever it was on the beach would see she was leaving and not follow.

Harry raced after her, grabbing a hold of the end of her cloak, stopping her progress.

"Please don't go. He wants you to stay."

A cry of salutation reached her on the wild wind. "Naomi! Wait!"

She tore her gaze from her brother to the approaching male. He was very tall and broad shouldered. The only man she knew who fitted that physique was Monsale. But he was shortly to be married; and right now, was probably spending the morning with his future in laws. He most certainly didn't have time to go wandering the beach.

Naomi shook her head. She must be imagining things, craving her heart's desire for one last time.

Her name came to her once more on the wind. "Naomi!"

As he drew closer, she simply stared. It was Monsale.

"I don't understand," she said.

Harry pulled her into his arms and gave her a hearty hug. "You will." He drew back and smiled at her. "Give him one last chance. He knows he has made an almighty mess of things. And also, what he stands in danger of losing."

"What do you mean? I am the one who has lost everything."

With that, Harry leaned in and gave her a quick peck on the cheek. "I hope to see you very soon." He wandered off in the direction of the castle, giving Monsale a wide berth as he went.

Her gaze settled back on the approaching Monsale. He was carrying something draped across his arms and striding with great purpose toward her. She stood, unable to move. A small voice in the back of her mind urged Naomi to run to him, but she refused to listen to its plea.

He is marrying Lady Euphemia. It wouldn't be right for me to throw myself at him.

Naomi would honor their long friendship today and be gracious in defeat. Hopefully, it would be the first step in the long healing process for her heart. She would learn to move forward with her own life. Perhaps one day, find another who would want her love.

When he finally got within a few yards of her, Monsale stopped. There were two objects in his arms. One was a large bunch of flowers. Beautiful white and pink damask roses. They must have come from the hothouse at the castle. The other was a long, broad edged sword.

Monsale bent and gently set the roses down on the sand. He then knelt, and with the sword held flat across both his palms, he raised his arms, offering the sword to her.

Naomi scowled. What on earth was he doing?

Intrigued, she stepped forward and came to him. "What is going on?"

He grinned up at her. "This is me offering my sword to you. I am conceding defeat. You win Naomi. The war is over."

"I...I don't understand," she stammered.

Monsale lay the sword next to the roses and got to his feet. With one large stride, he reached Naomi. She looked up as he towered over her.

"You win. I was stubborn and foolish. Thinking I could hold out and get you to marry me without ever offering my heart was wrong," he said.

Utterly perplexed at his words, Naomi continued to scowl up at him.

"I still don't understand what you are saying. I am the one who lost."

He shook his head. "Yes, and no. I have thought long and hard about this whole catastrophe for the best part of the last two days, and I've come to the realization that we both lost. And perhaps that was what had to happen in order for us to win."

"But Lady Euphemia..."

"Is somewhere on the road to Scotland this morning, traveling in Viscount Walsall's coach. She is with the man she loves. I can only hope that they have the good sense to head straight to Gretna Green and marry as soon as possible."

His fiancée had jilted him?

Monsale took a hold of Naomi's hand. "A short while ago, I announced to Lord and Lady Marshall that last night I decided I didn't want to marry Lady Euphemia. I also explained to them that in what can only be described as an astonishing coincidence, Viscount Walsall just happened to be passing Monsale Castle in the dark last night. He stopped and after offering for Euphemia, spirited her away. Suffice to say the Marshalls didn't take any of the news all that well. They left the castle just as I was crossing the dunes a short while ago."

Naomi swayed on her feet. *Monsale is not marrying Euphemia. Monsale is not…oh dear lord.*

Monsale slipped an arm around her waist and drew her into his embrace. Naomi met his gaze through a sheen of tears. "I'm sorry I was a stubborn ass. I held out thinking you would come to your senses. That you would understand why I didn't want to be on that list. But I miscalculated, and then it was all too late. I thought I had lost you."

He brushed a tender kiss on her lips. "I should never have asked Kitty to put the list together. There is, and always has been just one woman I wanted by my side. And that's you Naomi."

"Are you sure? You've kept me at arm's length for so long that I truly began to doubt it. You were and will always be my first choice in life. But it has to be the same for you."

"I've been a coward when it comes to love. With everything else in my life, I've always had control. I held back because I was afraid to trust someone with my heart. But if the way you have behaved over the past few days has taught me anything, it's that you are the only woman I know I can love."

She kissed him back. "You know I hate you for putting us through all this?"

A gentle nod was his reply.

His lips captured hers with a second kiss. He pulled her hard against him as he deepened the kiss and plundered her mouth. She surrendered, yielding everything he demanded of her. Allowing him to finally claim what had always been his —her love.

For the longest time, they stood kissing and holding one another. The rest of the world didn't exist. It was only them.

When Monsale finally released Naomi's lips, he lay her head against his chest, brushing his hand over her wind-swept hair. "I hurt you and for that, I shall always be sorry. I love you, Naomi."

She closed her eyes and sighed. Finally. All those long years waiting. Praying. Hoping. Hearing him say the words seemed almost surreal.

"Now what happens? You still need to marry, and you only have five days," she said.

He kissed the top of her head. "That's why I am here now. To talk to you. To confess all my sins."

❧

Over the years he had held on to the promise of finding his duchess and never having to reveal all the details of his sordid, dark past. But this was Naomi, and if he was serious about creating a loving marriage, he was going to have to tell her everything. As much as was possible.

"Come and sit with me, we need to talk," he said.

Picking up the roses, he handed them to Naomi. "These are for you. The best blooms from the hothouse. Grown here in Kent."

"They are stunning," she said.

He hated himself for having put that look of pained confusion on her face. For what his stubborn, determined heart had done to Naomi. It had refused to love.

I don't deserve you. But I will spend the rest of my life trying to be worthy.

Picking up his sword, Monsale guided Naomi to a small inlet, further away from the shore. It was out of the chilly wind and private. They sat on the dry sand, with Naomi still clutching the precious roses in her hands.

"What do you want to talk about?" she asked.

"I want to tell you a little more about the man that I am. There are things I have done in the past for which I am deeply ashamed. And also, there are some things which you have to accept I can never tell you. If you did know about them, your life wouldn't be safe."

She brushed her fingers over one of the pale pink petals. "I know you and your father were privateers."

He huffed. "You have no idea how much I wish that was the extent of things. Yes, we did have letters of mark from the British government which permitted us to conduct acts of war against England's enemies, but we went well beyond those agreements. We were pirates. I was running pirate ships out of Cable Bay, Bermuda by the time I was eleven. I am still wanted by both the Americans and the French for piracy and crimes on the high sea. And that is only a fraction of the wicked deeds I have done in my life."

There I have finally said it. I am more than just a rogue.

Lifting her head, she turned and met his gaze. "Why are you telling me this?"

"Because you should know before you agree to bind yourself to me. The rumors about me which you no doubt have heard over the years are more than likely true."

"But Harry was involved in much of those things, wasn't he?"

Monsale chuckled. "Your brother hasn't a clue as to half

the things I have done. He never really got his hands dirty. Whereas I have been up to my elbows in filth."

She shifted, setting the roses aside, and taking his hand. "You want me to know about the life you have led. Yes, that is something I need to know. What is more important for me, however, are your plans for the future. I want to know what sort of man the father of my children will be, and if you intend to change your ways. That is of course if you have it in mind to offer me marriage."

He had only a handful of days left in which to secure a wife. Time was of the essence. But Naomi had to be walking into this marriage with open eyes. To understand how things were and decide if she could live with a man who had never known a life outside of crime.

"Over the past year, and especially since Harry and George both married, I have been slowly moving away from the less savory side of things. Trying to set my business dealings on a more honest footing. When Stephen took on a wife and family, it made me realize I had to make those changes at a faster rate. All of us agreed that Stephen's brother Toby, shouldn't be raised around criminal activities."

If anyone had told him several years ago, that it would be a six-year-old boy who finally put paid to many of his dodgy dealings, Monsale would have laughed long and hard in their faces. But the innocent Toby Moore had compelled him to take stock of his life. To measure and assess his worth. He had found himself coming up well short. Unworthy of the Monsale title.

Reaching into his coat, he pulled out his pistol. Holding it by the end of the barrel he offered it to her. As soon as Naomi had taken it, he stuffed his hand into another pocket and withdrew a knife. She took that as well.

Harry had talked about the need for grand gestures, this was one of the most important of them. "I am laying my weapons aside. For you."

Naomi cleared her throat. "What about the knife you have strapped to your ankle?"

Oh.

He reached down and unstrapped the knife. When she continued to hold his gaze, Monsale sighed. Naomi really did have the measure of him. Reluctantly, he produced a second pistol and yet another knife from the deep pockets of his coat. He lay them on the sand, next to his sword.

"I think this might be the first time since I was a small child that I haven't had a weapon on my person. To tell you the truth I feel a little naked," he said.

Naomi quirked an eyebrow at his remark. "It is possible for one to get about life without being armed to the teeth. I promise to protect you from any and all harm."

He offered her his hand, intending that they head back to the castle. She shook her head. "Tell me what really happened with you and Lady Euphemia."

"Nothing. The night I danced with her at the ball…" He flinched as Naomi reached out and punched him hard on the arm. "Ow. What was that for?"

"For dancing with another woman. You cad. You held me at bay all those years and yet, you tripped the light fantastic with her."

If it weren't for the edge of pain in her voice, he would have laughed. She was jealous over him dancing with Lady Euphemia, a woman he had never intended to marry.

But he understood her anger. He had hurt Naomi. Humiliated her in front of other people. His friends and her family were all well aware of her attraction to him. At the time he had simply been paying her back for her refusing to put her name on the list and hadn't put much thought into what he was doing.

Avoiding the weapons, he moved, and knelt in front of Naomi. Taking her face in his hands, he leaned in close. "That was a selfish and thoughtless thing to do. I promise I will never knowingly hurt you ever again. And all my dances are now yours."

He captured her mouth in a warm, tender kiss. Their lips and tongues now moving in a slow, familiar embrace. Kissing Naomi was fast becoming his favorite pastime.

"What is to happen now? I mean since the wedding is off, you are still in a bind," asked Naomi when they finally broke the kiss.

Monsale was enjoying the simple pleasure of staring into Naomi's greenish blue eyes. He had always had a particular appreciation of the sharp intelligence which sparkled in them. With their foreheads pressed together, he was more than happy for this moment to continue.

But she was right. A wedding was still in order.

"That wedding might well have bitten the dust, but no one says we cannot have a different one."

He climbed to his feet, offering her his hand. "Come. Let you and I finally put all this other noise and nonsense behind us. Everyone else will be assembled at the castle, waiting for the marriage service. We shouldn't disappoint them."

A grinning Naomi placed her hand in his, and he helped her to stand. They were soon on their way back to Monsale Castle, the roses still cradled lovingly in her arms.

Monsale chanced a look back over his shoulder at the weapons he had left behind. The grand gesture having been delivered, there was no need to abandon them. He would send a servant back for them as soon as he got home.

Sharp weapons should never be left to go to waste.

Chapter Twenty-Two

The great hall of Monsale Castle was abuzz with activity and chatter. Servants were continually moving about, placing large pots and vases of roses all about the room. Pink silk curtains had been draped around the high windows. The proceedings for a wedding were continuing, and the mood was definitely romantic.

"I swear I saw Lord and Lady Marshall's travel coach leaving earlier. And no one seems to know where Lady Euphemia is," said Stephen.

Bridget, who was cradling baby Elizabeth Rose in her arms, Toby by her side, skimmed the room. "More importantly, where is Monsale? No bride. No groom. I have a horrible feeling that this wedding may not be going ahead."

Her husband leaned in and placed a tender kiss on his wife's cheek. He took a gurgling Elizabeth Rose from her and wrapped his daughter into the warmth of his jacket. Toby gave a friendly wave to the baby.

Harry and Alice entered the room; they were followed by Gus, Evangeline, George, and Jane. Behind them walked the Duke and Duchess of Redditch, baby Jonathan lay asleep in his grandfather's arms.

Bridget frowned. All the guests were here except for Lady Naomi Steele.

"I hope this day is not so terrible an ordeal for Naomi that she couldn't bear to come to the service. Poor girl, she had her heart set on marrying Monsale for such a long time. I just can't understand where it all went wrong."

The arrival of the local church minister dressed fully in his official robes set the hubbub of chatter to an even higher level. The question on everyone's lips.

"Where was Monsale?"

The Duke of Monsale's silver-haired steward Adan appeared in the doorway. He marched into the middle of the great hall; a large ebony staff held in his hand. When he reached the front of the room, he stopped, turned, and faced the gathering.

"His grace the Duke of Monsale!"

He rapped the staff on the stone floor, the sound of it echoing in the cavernous space.

All heads turned as Monsale strolled into the room. A hum of whispers quickly followed as the guests all took in the sight of Lady Naomi Steele, her hand held in his, as they walked side by side. She wore a pale pink gown with matching silk roses which trimmed the edge of the bodice. In her hair sat a dazzling diamond and ruby tiara.

Bridget and Alice exchanged a hopeful look. The Duchess of Redditch gasped and put her hand over her heart. "The Monsale tiara, oh Naomi."

Monsale led Naomi to the front of the room. "Thank you," said Monsale, as a smiling Adan stepped aside. The steward gave a nod. "Your grace."

Monsale slipped his hand from Naomi's and turned to her, bowing low. "My love."

Bridget promptly burst into tears.

"I expect you are all wondering what on earth has occurred this morning," said Monsale.

"That would be a large understatement," grumbled the Duke of Redditch.

Naomi held her hands together and laughed. Joy coursed through her whole body. The happiness, she had thought lost only a short time ago, now sparked once more to life. The only thing which shone brighter was the priceless Monsale tiara.

"Lady Euphemia and Lord Walsall have eloped to Scotland. They went with my blessing. I informed Lord and Lady Marshall of this development earlier this morning, and understandably, they decided to return to London immediately," announced Monsale.

There was not a dry eye in the house as a smiling Monsale went down on bended knee. "I love you, Naomi. You are my world. By refusing to accept our love, I hurt you. I am so, so terribly sorry to have made you suffer. When I finally came to understand how much I do love you, it made me see so many things through your eyes."

He loves me. Be still my beating heart.

"I love you too."

It was all she could manage.

"In front of everyone here today, I am declaring myself to you. Offering you a full partnership in my life. Lady Naomi Steele, love of my heart. Will you do me the greatest honor ever and be my wife? My duchess."

Naomi glanced at her mother. A tearful Kitty nodded. She knew how much this moment meant, how long her daughter had waited.

"Yes."

Cheers and applause erupted as Monsale got to his feet and hauled Naomi into his arms. He captured her lips, kissing her without restraint. She didn't care if her parents were watching, this moment was everything. They were both panting when they eventually drew apart.

He reached into his pocket and pulled out a piece of paper, then handed it to the priest.

"I think you should find the special license is all in correct order. Especially the names of the bride and groom."

Naomi's mouth opened and then closed. Monsale had arrived at the castle with the marriage license in hand. Her future husband sensibly avoided her gaze as it drilled into him.

You dirty, rotten, wonderful man.

"I should go back to the beach and get one of your pistols and shoot you," she said.

"I think it might be bad luck to murder the groom at his wedding. Especially before the service. Speaking of which, did you want to take some time with your mother now and prepare? I mean, I don't know what women do before weddings, but if you want..."

"No."

"What about talking to your parents?"

Naomi waved her father over. "Papa, will you give this marriage your blessing?"

The Duke of Redditch wrapped a fatherly arm around Naomi's shoulder. "Only if this truly makes you happy. Your mother and I have always said that love is more important than money. If you think Monsale has come to see the error of his ways, which it looks as if he has, then yes. I give you both my blessing."

Monsale bowed his head. "Your grace. I will do everything in my power to make Naomi's life one full of happiness."

The duke slapped his future son-in-law on the back. "Then get on with it."

As her father took his place once more alongside his wife, Naomi decided she wasn't going to waste another minute, she was more than ready. She turned to the minister; hands gently clasped together. Monsale joined her.

When the priest reached the part of the service where he asked if anyone present knew a reason why they shouldn't be lawfully married, a ripple of laughter rang through the room. The bride and groom both shook their heads.

Family and friends, heaven love them were the very worst. And the very best.

"I suggest we throw them all out the moment the wedding is over. None of them are getting fed," whispered Monsale.

Naomi shot him a conspiratorial look. "I hope you retrieved your weapons from the beach. Because if you try to get between Gus and food, there will be a riot."

The rest of the wedding service went without incident. An emotional Naomi struggled to back the tears when Monsale opened an elegant silver box containing six gold wedding bands of different sizes all arranged neatly on a red velvet cushion.

"I wasn't sure of your size," he said.

After trying several rings, they found one which fit perfectly. Monsale slipped it on Naomi's finger.

"It's a little late, for this, but you may now kiss the bride," said the priest.

As the bride and groom locked lips, a roar of applause and cheers rang through the hall. Adan struck the staff on the floor once more and cried. "Huzzah!"

Naomi gazed lovingly into the eyes of her new husband. "I will do everything in my power to be the wife and duchess you need. To make you proud of me."

Monsale brushed his hand over her cheek. "My love, you are already more than I could have ever hoped to find in a wife. I am so very proud of you Naomi. You stood your ground and refused to settle for being anything other than my first and only choice."

He wrapped her gently in his arms and whispered. "This is forever."

"Rome has fallen!" cried Harry.

"All hail Naomi, Lady Monsale," added Alice.

I am a duchess. But more importantly I am Monsale's wife.

Hand in hand they went to receive the congratulations of their friends and family.

Chapter Twenty-Three

The wedding breakfast went on all afternoon, Gus made a fair fist of eating his own body weight, which had Evangeline rubbing his stomach and informing her husband that he was going on a soup diet as soon as they returned to France.

Slipping with ease into her new role of castle hostess, Naomi inquired as to whether any of the guests were going to need supper. Kitty shook her head.

"Your father and I won't require food. We are going to start back on the road to London shortly, staying overnight in Faversham. I think Harry and Alice are going to do the same."

After a hurried conversation among the rest of the guests, it was soon decided that the other members of the rogues of the road and their families would also be making their way home. Supper would not be needed.

"You don't have to go, there is plenty of room at the castle," offered Monsale.

George placed a hand on the groom's brow. "Monsale playing at host, my dear boy, are you coming down with something?"

Monsale batted his hand away and laughed. "No. But this is my— I mean Naomi and my wedding day, we thought you might want to stay."

George leaned in. "Yes, your wedding day. And tonight, is your wedding night. You don't need a house full of people disturbing your privacy. From someone who ruined his own wedding night, trust me on this."

Out of the corner of his eye, Monsale caught sight of his bride. She was giving a heartfelt and quite emotional farewell to her parents.

Perhaps George is right. If Naomi is not having to worry about guests and their accommodations, she will be more relaxed this evening.

There had been so much happening this day, Monsale had almost forgotten about their wedding night. Of the moment when he and Naomi would finally become man and wife. He had a sudden thought; the wedding had been unexpected. And Naomi had not spent any time with her mother before the service.

I do so hope Kitty has had the talk with her daughter at some point.

He had no experience when it came to bedding virgins.

This is Naomi. You love her. Just be gentle. Answer any of her questions and take things slowly. Tonight, should be about her.

She was his to love and protect. And tonight, would be the perfect opportunity for him to show her what that really meant. To guide her safely from innocence to well sated wife.

He scrubbed his hand over his mouth, surprised to discover that he was actually a touch nervous. In the past, he hadn't ever had to worry about his performance in the bedroom, but those had been meaningless encounters.

This was Naomi, and it meant everything. Tonight, would be the first time for them to come together as husband and wife.

A soft smile of anticipation sat on Monsale's lips as he went in search of a stiff, fortifying drink.

Chapter Twenty-Four

Naomi gave one final wave to the departing travel coach before turning back to the main castle keep. The last of the wedding guests had gone. Now it was just her and Monsale. And the night ahead.

She swallowed nervously. Her belly was already full of butterflies. Her fingers had a slight tremble to them.

Kitty had sat her down and had the chat many years ago, when Naomi's monthly courses had first begun. The duchess was a practical woman, determined that her daughter should understand what was happening to her body.

Armed with a basic knowledge of the act, and a few years of listening to gossip at parties and balls, Naomi wasn't a complete novice about things. But hearing and reading was an entirely different prospect to actually experiencing it.

When Bridget went up to her and Stephen's room to put Elizabeth Rose down for a mid-afternoon nap, Naomi had followed in her friend's wake. As soon as she stepped into the room, she closed the door behind her.

"Sorry to disturb, but I wondered if I could have a word. About tonight."

Bridget gave an understanding smile in reply. "What do you want to know? Or should I ask, what is it that you already know?"

Being close friends, they had talked enough about things over the years, but Naomi still had questions.

"How do you know if it is good? And what am I supposed to do?"

"If Monsale is as kind with you as I hope he will be, there will be no mistaking whether you enjoy it or not. Let him show you the way. And in time when you feel more confident, then you can take the lead."

She took a hold of Naomi's hand and gave it a soft pat. "Just relax and remember this is the first night of your whole marriage. Don't put too much pressure on yourself to be someone you are not. Monsale loves you for you, let him show it."

Naomi frowned. She had been hoping for something a little more concrete, a tip or two that would set Monsale on fire with desire for her.

Maybe she is right. If I just let things happen and let him guide me.

"I'm sorry Naomi, that was all a little vague. From what I can remember of my wedding night, with my first husband, he took care of me, and I survived it. Within days all I wanted was to be in bed with him, and for us to be making love. It's a pity our marriage eventually failed, but sex wasn't the reason," said Bridget.

"Thank you. I must confess to being a little nervous. When I woke this morning, I was expecting to be a bystander at today's proceedings, not the center of them."

"He loves you. And believe me the greatest thing a man wants to do for the woman in his life is to give her pleasure." Bridget grinned. "Because if you are enjoying the marital bed, it will make it easier for him to get you naked and in it.

Believe me, Monsale will be doing his utmost to make sure you get a taste for his touch."

Heat burned on Naomi's cheeks. Her wild imaginings of sex were about to become very real.

Chapter Twenty-Five

With their guests now gone, Monsale led Naomi back into the main castle building and up the winding stairs to what was now their bedroom. When they reached the door, he stopped and let go of her hand. "We could go for a walk if you like, or we could spend some time in our room and then ring for supper later. Whatever makes you feel more comfortable."

Naomi toyed with the gold wedding band on her finger. "I don't think my nerves could handle a walk. And to be honest, my knees are a little shaky," she replied.

Monsale came and stood face to face with her, their noses barely touching. A shiver slid down her spine as he began to slowly rub his nose against hers. Such a simple act and yet, it was so profoundly intimate. Naomi had long craved for matters between her and Monsale to be this way. So, loving. So, real.

He took a gentle hold of her hands. His were warm and strong. "Don't ever be afraid of me, Naomi. Or of us and what we have. I want our first time together to be a wonderful experience for you."

"Bridget said you would make sure it was good."

"You spoke to Bridget today?"

"Yes. We have always been close. She and I have shared many private conversations over the years. Through the sad times with her late husband. And I was her confidante when she and Stephen first began their relationship. Talking to her this afternoon helped to somewhat alleviate my concerns."

He bent and kissed her lips.

"So, are you comfortable for us to become lovers? I won't ever make you do anything you don't want."

"Yes." She had dreamed of this moment for many years. Had laid in her bed at night, touching herself, imagining that the hands which stroked her heat were Monsale's. Nothing was going to stop her from experiencing the real thing. Of finally knowing what it was to be with him.

Monsale opened the door to their room and ushered Naomi inside. He closed the door and turned the key in the lock. "Just to make sure we are not disturbed. The staff here are not used to having a duchess in residence."

Naomi's gaze took in the deep crimson coverlet draped over the bed. Then the matching curtains, and gold and red striped woolen carpet. Everything in the room was lush, ornate. It spoke of wealth, and power.

Monsale screwed up his face. "I had a decorator come up from London and create this look a few years ago. I must confess I was going through my '*I am monarch of all I survey*' phase and probably took things a little too far when it came to the color scheme. If you feel the need to make changes, please go ahead."

She glanced around the room, taking it all in. "I like it. The rest of the castle is stone and wood, whereas this room has a warmth about it. This is our room. If we decide on any alterations either here or at Monsale House, we should do it together."

Naomi had observed her parents' marriage, how they negotiated their way through the long years of being a couple. The example of give and take was one she hoped to follow. The duke and duchess had always shared a bedroom. Even when they were going through the occasional rough patch that Kitty told her every couple experienced, they still slept together. They worked through their problems and differences. She intended that her and Monsale's marriage would be built on the same firm foundations.

But right now, Naomi didn't want to think about furnishings or other people. This time was for her and Monsale. Taking a deep breath, she stepped forward, lifted her head, and met his gaze.

"Make love to me."

Monsale's expression changed to one of loving regard. He gave a nod of understanding. There would be plenty of time for them to discuss mundane matters, but this moment was all about the two of them. Of sealing their union and becoming one.

Their mouths met in a soft, tender kiss. Naomi slipped her hands inside Monsale's jacket, her fingers gripping the sides of his waistcoat. She groaned as he deepened the kiss.

Her mind brought up memories of that morning in the carriage, of how primal Monsale's touch had been. She had been in no doubt that he had been on the verge of claiming her that day. If she had offered herself to him, he would have taken everything and more.

His lips drifted from her mouth, tracing slow kisses across her cheek. When he reached her ear, he whispered. "I want to know what you like. Tell me, Naomi, wife of mine, have you touched yourself when you are alone in your bed?"

Heat burned on her cheeks, and she lowered her head. She had never spoken of those moments with anyone else. Just the thought of her secret desires set her mouth to dry.

"I." She swallowed. This was so personal. So private.

Monsale's lusty chuckle sent a pulse of heat coursing through her body. It settled in her aching core. Did he have any idea what this was doing to her?

"Now Naomi, we can't be keeping secrets from one another. I shall tell you everything you wish to know, but in return, you have to—no you *must* let me enjoy every single naughty one of yours."

Placing a finger under her chin, he lifted her face. Naomi shyly met his gaze. "If you like I can go first. Tell you one of my dark secrets."

She nodded.

"The reason why I refused every time you asked me to dance with you, is because I knew if you were close, I wouldn't be able to control myself. My manhood would go hard, and you would finally know that I desired you."

Her eyes grew wide at hearing his confession. All those nights when he had said no, he had been longing to say yes. Monsale had kept his distance because she was pure temptation. Another pulse of lust coursed through her.

"I see."

"Ah, but what you don't know is that after I refused you, I would go home, lay on my bed and think about you. Of how wonderful it would be to hold you. To have you in my arms. To touch and kiss every inch of your naked body."

"Oh."

Her breath grew ragged hearing her husband confess his secret longing for her. It was thrilling. She wanted to know more.

"Did the thought of me make you pleasure yourself, husband of mine?"

It was a bold question. One she had never imagined ever asking a man, but Naomi couldn't resist. She had to know if Monsale had ached for her the same as she had yearned for him.

"Every single time. You are the woman I have lain awake and thought of for countless nights."

A whoosh of air escaped her lips. She had been on his mind all those years.

Tell him.

"I touch myself and think of you. It's not my hand stroking my body, it's yours. The nights when you have turned your cool, Duke of Monsale bearing on me are the worst, or should I say— the best. Without fail, I have gone home every time and thought of you ravishing me. Bringing me to me climax over and over."

She looked away, not wanting to meet his eyes. This conversation was breaking down all the barriers, the high walls, they had built to keep each other out. They were now standing in the crumbling ruins, finally seeing one another.

"Look at me Naomi," he said. She shyly lifted her head. The warm, loving expression on her husband's face a sight which she hoped he would always have for her. "Let's take this slow. If at any time you feel unsure, just let me know."

Her fingers settled on the buttons of his waistcoat. She didn't want it too slow, nor did she intend to be the passive one in this moment. With a twist, she flicked open the top button.

"Keep going," he said.

The rest of the buttons met the same fate, after which Monsale shrugged out of his jacket. The waistcoat followed it to the floor.

"And now the shirt if you would be so kind, your grace," she said.

He laughed. "Terribly formal, but my wish is your command, your grace."

Crossing his arms, he bunched up the sides of his linen shirt and pulled it over his head. Naomi gasped. Across his chest and stomach were dotted various markings. He glanced down at himself. "Ah. I forgot about those."

She lay her fingers on the black outline of a swallow, tracing the edges of the wings. "What are these?"

"I wasn't lying when I said I was a pirate at an early age. I got these tattoos in Nassau on my eleventh birthday. Hurt like the devil, but I was determined not to cry. You can't command men if they think you are soft."

He placed his hand over hers. "They are only ink on my skin, symbols of a time when I could have become something else. Tonight, is about us, our future. And the man I want to be for you."

"Yes. And the woman I want to be for you too," replied Naomi.

She was done with waiting. The time had come for her to be brave and claim what she had yearned for all those years.

Releasing her hand from his, Naomi took a step back. Her fingers worked quickly to loosen the ties of her gown. She kicked off her silver slippers. Then, taking a deep breath, she lifted the skirts of her gown and drew it over her head. It dropped to the floor.

When Monsale reached for her, she gave him a saucy shake of the head. No. She wanted to do this on her own. To strip completely naked for him.

His lust filled gaze tracked her every move. "Naomi," he whispered.

Her fingers touched the top of her stockings and Monsale instantly held up his hand.

"No. Leave them on."

"Why?"

"Because I have fantasized about our first time more than you can imagine. Over time things have become quite detailed in my mind. You wearing your stockings is definitely something I need. Please, Naomi. For me," he said, his voice gruff with hunger.

Naomi let her hands fall away. "I would do anything for you, my love. Just don't make me wait."

Monsale quickly toed off his boots. But when he reached for the placket of his trousers and slipped the buttons open, Naomi had her first real moment of doubt. His erection bobbed free, and she gasped. It was larger than she had imagined it would be, and thick.

Just trust him. He will know what to do.

Her bravado was beginning to falter by the time the last of her undergarments hit the carpet, but fortunately, she didn't have time to let shyness set in. Monsale scooped her up in his arms and carried Naomi over to the bed. He lay her down on the coverlet, then climbed on after her.

"I love you," he said. His words warm and reassuring, gave Naomi all the encouragement she needed.

Their mouths fused in a scorching kiss, tongues tangling. She was greedy, aching with need, wanting nothing more than to feel his hands on her heated flesh. To give herself to this man.

"So beautiful," he whispered as his gaze settled on her naked breasts. "I can't begin to tell you the number of times I have stared at the bodice of your evening gown, all the while mentally tugging down the top and baring you to my sight. And while I have imagined that your nipples would be magnificent, the reality is beyond words. May I touch them?"

The reverence in his voice was so profound. This was the real Andrew McNeal, her Monsale. The man no other woman would ever know.

Her rosy buds hardened into peaks, desperate for his touch. "I think I might die if you don't. So, yes please."

Naomi shivered as Monsale brushed a thumb lightly back and forth over her flushed, pink skin. He bent his head and taking one of her sensitive buds into his mouth, gently sucked. Her back arched off the bed. This was heaven.

"Oh god…". Naomi gasped as she speared her fingers into her husband's hair, desperate to hold him in place.

"You like me doing that, good. I want to know everything that pleasures you, my love."

Then he went back to teasing her breasts. Licking, sucking, and to her, delighted surprise lightly nipping them. If he was this skilled when it came to simply toying with her nipples, she dared not think how masterful he would be when it came to the act of lovemaking.

She released him from her grip and as Monsale lifted his head, he asked. "Are you ready to take the next step?"

Naomi nodded. "I am yours. I want you to explore and lay claim to every inch of me. And I want to do the same to you."

His knee pushed her legs apart, and Naomi took a deep breath, trying to calm her nerves. All thoughts of relaxation quickly fled her mind as Monsale pressed his thumb deep into her sex and began to stroke. "Monsale," she groaned.

Her head fell back against the pillow as the first wave of exquisite sexual release washed over her. When he drew his fingers back, they brushed over her swollen bud, sending sparks of pleasure to her brain. She had been a fool to worry about her first time, he knew exactly what he was doing.

A sensual game of tease and reward quickly ensued. Every time Naomi let out a sob of need, Monsale rewarded her with a kiss and soft words of encouragement. "That's it, show me how much you want this, my love."

"It feels so good," she whimpered.

"I want your body to burn with desire every time I touch you. For you to crave the climax that only I can give you. As my wife, you have the right to demand it of me. Whenever and wherever you want it, you only have to ask. I am yours in all things."

"Take me. Make me yours," she begged.

Monsale withdrew his hand from her throbbing, wet core. The hard length of his cock pressed against her inner thigh as he shifted and settled between her legs. Naomi was as ready as she would ever be for this, their first time.

"I will be as gentle as I can," he said.

Naomi closed her eyes as Monsale slowly pushed in, stretching her sheath. There was a small pinch, and then the wonderful sensation of him being inside her.

"Oh, my god. Monsale," she groaned.

He slid his cock most of the way back out, then stilled. "Are you alright my love?"

She slapped her hands on his hips and pulled him toward her. "Never better. Now make it good. Make me forget all those nights when I only had my hand and thoughts of you to bring me to climax."

He came back to her, rocking his hips slowly in and out, grinding against her swollen nib as his thick erection filled her once more. They soon created a sweet rhythm. Monsale plunging into her heat, while Naomi met his every thrust with her sobs and cries of need.

The tension built to a familiar peak, and she knew she was close.

Opening her eyes, Naomi looked deep into the silver warmth of the man she had loved forever. "Don't hold back, I want it harder. Claim me. Take it all."

Monsale lifted her stocking clad leg over his hip then thrust back into her wet heat. The angle and magnificent depth of penetration had Naomi seeing stars. He now rode her faster and harder, until on one final, exquisite thrust, he slammed deep into her sex and Naomi shattered on a scream.

"Monsale!"

She was still pulsing, riding the crest of her climax, when he stilled and let out a long shuddering groan of satisfaction. Monsale collapsed on top of her.

It took a minute or so for Naomi to finally find the strength to lift her legs and wrap them around him. She held her husband tight.

"That was better than I could have ever imagined, you were magnificent, my love," she whispered.

He kissed the side of her neck. In the dark his words brought her to tears.

"I love you. I am yours, now and forever."

Chapter Twenty-Six

Monsale rolled over in the middle of the night, and immediately sensed something was wrong. He and Naomi had fallen asleep in one another's arm, but instead of the warm, supple body of his wife being pressed against him, he found only empty sheets.

Naomi was gone.

Throwing back the covers, he leapt out of bed, stopping to grab his pistol from under the mattress. He glanced at it. Having a loaded weapon in the bedroom might be something he had to reconsider. Old habits would take time to change.

Quickly dressing, he stuffed his feet into his boots. Life had taught him to take a minute longer and make sure he was ready for anything before heading out into possible danger.

He crept silently along the hallway, grateful that the lanterns which hung along its length lit the way.

Where is she?

Monsale searched room after room, cursing the castle for the sheer number of them. After he had poked his head into every room on this level of the castle, he headed upstairs. More fruitless searching followed. He was on the verge of ringing the bell and rousing all the staff from their beds to help him hunt for his wife, when a light shining through the door of the room at the end of the hall caught his eye.

He hurried to it.

"Naomi?"

The pistol was in his hand, ready for any trouble.

"Yes?"

"Are you alone? And are you safe?"

His wife appeared from out of the library, a large book clutched to her chest.

"Yes, to both questions."

Her gaze fell on the weapon in his hand. "What's going on?"

Monsale ushered her back into the room, setting the gun down on the nearest table. He frowned at the book. "What are you doing in here? I reached for you in our bed, and you were gone. You had me worried."

It was strange to hear those words coming from his own lips, but it was the truth. Since opening his heart to Naomi, he was finding himself having to come to terms with all manner of new emotions. Worrying over her was one of them.

He could also admit to a touch of concern over finding her gone from their bed. When they had made love, she had been pure poetry in his arms. He was sure her cry of completion was real. But a grain of doubt still sat in the back of his mind.

"I couldn't sleep, so I decided to come looking in the library for old books. I was hoping to find information about the fealty oath," she replied.

Monsale gently took the book from out of Naomi's hands and set it on the table next to the pistol. Slipping his arms around her, he pulled his wife into his embrace. She lifted her head, offering her mouth for his easy kiss.

"Are you alright? I mean after tonight."

She nodded, a soft smile on her lips. "Yes. Tonight, was wonderful. I plan to take you up on your offer of us making love whenever and wherever I want."

This woman. She humbled him with her open affection. He had been a fool to waste the past few years, denying his growing attraction to her. Keeping her at arm's length. Hurting her.

And I almost lost her.

"I can come back to bed if you need me now," she said. Her words a clear invitation. If you want me.

"Soon, my love. But first I wish to know more about your search. Did you uncover anything?"

"Unfortunately, not. I did manage to find a little bit about the first Duke of Monsale. The one who picked the wrong side in the battle. Robert McNeal. From what I read in that book I can see where you get your skills for business dealings from. He apparently swindled a lot of the original Monsale wealth out of other people."

He laughed. His father had always found that particular story to be of great amusement. The McNeal bloodline was full of rogues and dirty dealers.

"Didn't you ever wonder why a duke from Kent had a Scottish surname? It's because he sold a massive tract of land in the highlands to a gullible English lord, in exchange for the land around here in Deal. Legend has it that the other chap was too embarrassed at being taken for a fool to ever make a fuss about it."

The thought of his ancestor pulled Monsale up short. He and the rest of the family had known the history of their lands, yet no one had ever made mention of the oath ceremony. There had to be a record of it somewhere. For the story to have been handed on down the years.

Six hundred years ago, this sort of thing would have been written on parchment. A document like that probably wouldn't have survived the centuries.

His forebears must have had a way to share the knowledge.

Apart from the last two dukes, his father and uncle, the

rest of the Dukes of Monsale were all buried in the family crypt, here at Monsale Castle. A place where they had lived and died.

Now there is a thought. What if the record of the oath is in the crypt?

He glanced at Naomi's thin night attire. It was tempting to take her back to bed and make love to her once more, but since his wife had made the effort to follow up on the oath, he should support her. A gentle smile crept to his lips.

My wife.

"How about we go back to our room, and you can put something warmer on. I am thinking that the next place we should search is the family crypt," he said.

Naomi's eyes lit up. "A midnight treasure hunt. How exciting. This is the best wedding night present you could have given me."

"What about?"

He got a cuff over the ear for his cheeky impertinence. Naomi wagged a finger at him. "You are a saucy duke, and I shall have to punish you later for it."

Promise. Please.

After returning to their room where Naomi dressed and put on her cloak, they headed down to the main floor of the castle. Monsale pointed to a narrow set of steps set against the far wall of the great hall.

"I hope you are not scared of spiders," he said, taking a burning lantern down from off the wall.

The last time he had ventured down those stairs, he had been forced to fight his way through a labyrinth of cobwebs.

She shook her head. "No. I have many brothers, and all have at one time, or another subjected me to jests involving spiders, bugs, and mice. If I had an issue with any of those things, I should have perished from fright long ago."

Naomi might have no problems with things that crawled and scurried, but the dark wasn't her favorite place. Taking the lantern, she held it high above the topmost step and peered into the inky black of the stone staircase.

"We could always leave it until morning," she said.

Her husband leaned in close behind and whispered in her ear. "Where would the fun be in that? Just imagine in the years to come, you will be able to tell our children that you went on a grand adventure into the crypt."

"Or I could just tell them that their father did, while I stayed in the warmth of our bed because only a ninny would venture down into a dark dangerous place in the middle of the night."

A hot kiss was placed on her neck, followed by a teasing nip of her earlobe.

"But you are a McNeal now, we fear nothing."

I really should have pushed him to take me back to bed.

There was no getting out of it. "Alright, but you lead the way. If a big hairy beastie from the dark ages is lurking in the blackness, he will eat you first."

Monsale gave a harrumph of disgust and took the lantern from her hands.

"No beasties in Monsale Castle would dare. Besides, we feed them regularly."

Holding on to the back of her husband's coat, Naomi followed him down the stairs. Down. Down they went. The steps seemed to go on forever.

"The Steele family crypt is mostly above ground, with only a dozen steps leading down into the earth, which in my opinion is far more civilized," she said.

"Yes, but you don't have a six-hundred-and-fifty-year-old castle. Correction, you do since you are now a McNeal, but no, the Dukes of Redditch don't, the poor dears."

She was tempted to take him to task over the insult to her family, but the warmth in Monsale's voice when he mentioned that she was now a McNeal had Naomi blinking back a sudden tear. He really was her husband. After all they had been through it was still hard to accept that they were actually married.

A splash echoed in the darkness as Monsale's boots hit water. He stopped and Naomi came up flush against his back. "We have reached the main crypt," he announced.

"Where is the water coming from?"

"Take a breath, smell the sea saltwater. The high tide washes in between two of the low dunes. It comes into this space most days, and especially on king tides. That's why you won't find anything crawling about on the floor."

"Including me," she grumbled.

Monsale hung the lantern on a high hook. It bathed much of the small space in a pale eerie light. It was enough to be able to make out the various stone sarcophagi, and two large marble tablets. He pointed at the tablets. "Those are for my father and uncle. They are not buried here. I don't know what happened to James's body, and after the incident with the frigate, I dare not return to Bermuda to find out. We buried William at sea."

He had rarely mentioned his family over the years, but the edge of pain in his voice was unmistakable. Monsale might have been a strong-minded boy when he arrived in England, but he was still an orphan. A young lad left all alone in the world.

Naomi would be forever grateful for the kindness her parents had shown to Monsale. She dreaded to think what sort of man he may have eventually become without their steady hand helping to steer him away from the darkest life of villainy. He may well have been a lifelong criminal, but he wasn't evil. He had done shameful things, but there was now hope for Monsale to turn away from his past and embrace an honest existence.

I want to help you become the sort of man your children will be proud to call papa.

Naomi touched a hand to his coat sleeve. "They may not have made it back to England, but you gave your father and uncle a place here in the family crypt. To all intents and purposes, they are both here at home."

Monsale bowed his head. She slipped an arm around him, nuzzling into his shoulder as he drew her to him.

"I am sorry, Naomi. Sorry for all those years I kept my distance. I knew you would understand my family. That it would take a woman such as you, my love, to bring my heart peace. I just didn't know how to do it. To reach out."

"I know. That's why I never gave up on you."

They stood for a time, simply holding one another in the dull light. Words didn't need to be spoken. Two souls joined as one, understanding. Forgiving.

When the lamp gave a flicker, Monsale stirred. "We had better find Robert McNeal's sarcophagus before the flame blows out. Climbing those steps in the dark is not something I wish either of us to have to do."

They found Robert's resting place in the far corner of the crypt. The first duke had clearly expected his line to continue for many years and had made room for his future descendants to join him when they finally came to the end of their life's journey.

Naomi peered over the top of the sarcophagus. It had markings on it, but they were faded and hard to read. Ignoring the dust and sea grime, she climbed up. With her slippers perched on the bottom lip of the dais on which the coffin sat, she leaned over.

"I think its Latin," she said.

Monsale sighed. "I bloody hate Latin. When my father tried to get me to learn it, I refused. I couldn't see the point. It's a dead language. I convinced him to let my tutor teach me French instead. That was much more useful."

She could just imagine how her new husband had used his skills with the French language during the war. Harry had let slip enough clues for Naomi to have a pretty good idea as to what he and the rest of the rogues of the road had got up during their work for the crown.

And now the Prince Regent was doing his best to take Monsale's title and lands.

So much for rewarding loyalty.

"Yes, well, fortunately for us, my father was insistent on all of his children learning Latin. Mama thought the same thing about it being dusty and boring, but Papa wouldn't bend. He said it meant we were more than just wealthy farmers," she replied.

She brushed her hand over the nearest line of the markings and racked her brains trying to remember all the rules.

"*Hic jacet Robertus.* Well, it looks like we have the right coffin."

Her gaze roamed over the rest of the markings. "And here are some Roman numerals. Gosh, Robert lived to a ripe old age. Ninety-three years."

Resting her hands on the top of the stone sarcophagus, she sighed. "It's only got details about him and his life."

She righted herself and turned to Monsale. "Where is Robert's duchess?"

He looked around, checking the various stone sarcophagi which had been placed either side of Robert's. "I don't know."

His head lifted, and he stared at the wall behind the coffin. Naomi followed his gaze. She caught sight of an elegant statue of a woman clad in a gown with a belt around her waist. In the poor light she hadn't noticed the figure. Its hands were resting on the end of the duke's sarcophagus.

Naomi climbed down from the dais and lifting her skirts, waded through the water and over to the statue.

"Could you please bring the lantern closer?" she said.

Monsale quickly retrieved the lamp from the wall and brought it over. He held it high above Naomi while she examined the stonework. Her fingers touched the woman's belt. There were words etched into it.

"Ah! The answer is always with the woman. This is a fealty oath. *Promitto in fidem meam, quod ego in posterum fidelem.*"

"What does that mean?"

"I promise on my faith that I will in the future be faithful to the lord. There is more, but we might need to get pen, ink, and paper, so I can write it all down."

Robert's duchess. While she didn't know the woman's name, an important detail Naomi was determined to rectify, she clearly held a strong clue as to what the oath of fealty involved.

"I would bet this is a statue of Robert's wife, and that she is probably buried with him. That's why she doesn't have her own sarcophagus."

Naomi knew what she had to do.

I must transcribe the oath exactly word for word.

Knowing the Prince of Wales, he would demand that it be word-perfect. The last thing she and Monsale needed was for them to lose it all over a mere technicality.

Monsale lowered the lantern. "I tell you what. Let's head upstairs. We will come back in the morning with more light. Then you can take your time to write it all down."

Disappointment stirred within. It was dark. It was cold and wet. And yet, she was having one of the best moments of her life unraveling the mystery of the oath.

Her husband's strong arm wrapped around her waist, it, coupled with his kiss on the back of her neck settled any thoughts that Naomi might have had to protest.

"Yes, well, Robert and his duchess have been down here for almost six hundred years, so I don't expect they are going anywhere during the next few hours," she said.

"Come on wife. It's time we went back to bed."

Naomi rose on her toes, placing a tender kiss on his lips. "You had better not be planning on going to sleep husband. As I recall you offered to show me all the ways of love making. And I know enough from my friends that we have barely scratched the surface."

Nearing the steps, Monsale stopped and lifted the lantern. Naomi's gaze fell on a patch of the wall. It was solid gray, all except for one stone. It was white, and unlike the rest of the oddly shaped pieces, a perfect square.

He pressed his hand against it, and to her surprise the stone popped out. Monsale pulled on it and a small chest followed. The stone had been attached to the front of it, forming a clever disguise.

"Hold this," he said, handing her the lantern.

While she held the light, he opened the box and peeked inside. The unmistakable glint of gold caught Naomi's eye.

"What is it?"

"Spanish coins. Doubloons. I brought these with me when I left Bermuda. It's another of the secret treasures I have maintained over the years. This one is meant for Adan as his retirement fund, but he knows I like to check on it every once in a while. Just to make sure it is still here."

He closed the chest and placed it back in the wall, pressing the stone to lock it into place.

Naomi handed him the lamp. "I have a feeling I've a lifetime of surprises ahead of me."

Monsale bent and captured her mouth in a long, lingering kiss. "Come back to bed and let me show you what I can do with my tongue and lips. I want to hear you scream again."

Her skin burning with lust, her nipples hardened with the need for his attention, Naomi followed her husband upstairs.

"You are right, the oath can wait until morning."

Chapter Twenty-Seven

O*ath Day*

As the sun rose over a sleepy London, Monsale thrust deeply into his wife's welcoming body one last time and let out a long groan as he reached his sexual release. "I will never get enough of you."

He leaned back on his elbows, his heart fit to burst as he took in Naomi's sweet grin of satisfaction. Her fingers brushed the red rose he had tucked behind her ear when they had stolen into the hot house a short time earlier.

He had never been one for being awake at this time of the day, but Naomi had roused him half an hour earlier, insisting that he make love to her amongst the roses. She had informed him that the big old, daybed where they lay was fast becoming her favorite place for them to enjoy the pleasure of early morning sexual congress. With the promise of a warm, sated wife beneath him, Monsale wasn't about to deny her request.

"I love it in here. The scent of the roses does something to me," she said.

"Really? And what's that?"

She bit down on her bottom lip, and his cock stirred to life once more. Her lips were swollen from his kisses, her cheeks still flushed with passion. He had never seen such a beautiful sight. This woman was his world.

You are more than I ever thought I would know in a woman. My wife. My lover.

"It's the colors, the light, and the aroma. They make my core clench, and my mouth water. If you get what I mean," she said.

Monsale stared at her soft, pliant lips. He knew exactly what she meant. Naomi was a fast study when it came to marital relations. Every time he gave her roses, she dropped to her knees and took him into her mouth.

I wish I had time this morning to lay her down on a bed of petals.

"I promise we shall indulge your desires as soon as we return home from Carlton House," he said.

Naomi sighed. "Yes, I suppose we had better bathe and dress. I want to check the words of the oath one more time before we leave."

He rolled off his wife and got to his feet. She took his offered hand. "The last thing we want is to make a mistake with it. Not after all we have been through."

Word of their marriage had been kept secret upon their return to London, but now Monsale couldn't wait to see Prinny's face when he saw the new Duchess of Monsale kneeling beside him.

Their carriage drew up inside the rear mews of Carlton House. The sight of his wife as she stepped out, took Monsale's breath away.

The bodice of her golden gown caressed her beautiful curves. The rose-embroidered skirt flared at her hip, then flowed to the floor. A gold hair clip added just the right touch of noble elegance to the stylish chignon in which Naomi's light-brown hair had been set. A gold lace choker sat around her throat. She was stunning. Every inch, the Duchess of Monsale.

And to think I nearly lost you.

Monsale checked his jacket and gold-patterned waistcoat. They had deliberately coordinated their outfits. Side by side, they looked exactly what they were, a strongly bound couple.

Once inside the prince regent's private residence they were shown upstairs to an antechamber. Prinny might not yet be king, but he had already established a formal throne room in which he received guests. The doors of the throne room opened, and a royal footman loudly announced. "Their graces the Duke and Duchess of Monsale."

Prinny rose from his chair as they entered. His disapproving gaze tracked Naomi's every step as she approached.

At the exact right moment, she stopped and dipped into a deep curtsy. Its elegance reflecting both her family lineage and the hours of practice she had put in the previous day, under Kitty's watchful eye. His wife had done everything she could to make today a success.

"I see you managed to conjure up a bride, Monsale. I suppose congratulations are in order," said the prince. The tone of suspicion and disappointment in his voice was unmistakable.

"Thank you, your highness. While Lady Naomi and I have had a private understanding for some time, she was gracious enough to move our wedding plans forward to meet with your command."

The prince waved Monsale's words away. "Well, let's get on with it." His tone was that of bare interest, but the sly, conceited smile on his lips betrayed the prince. Monsale may well have taken a wife, but he still had to swear the oath of fealty. And get it right.

You think you have the measure of us.

Monsale glanced over at Naomi, and she gave a nod. Lifting her skirts, she slowly lowered herself to the floor, settling on her knees. Her husband knelt beside her, and after a short pause, they began "I promise on my faith, that I am in the future, to be faithful..."

A grinning Prince of Wales held up his hand. "The oath that Robert McNeal and his duchess swore was in Latin, not English. If you cannot recite it word-perfect in its original form, then you fail. And you forfeit. Everything."

Monsale lifted his head just in time to see the prince give a look of supreme smugness to his private secretary. It was clear he thought he had won.

"I hope you brought the keys to the front door of Monsale House with you. After today, you won't be needing them," said the prince.

Prinny was crowing in anticipation of his victory before the battle had barely begun. To Monsale's mind, that was a foolish mistake. One which he had made others pay dearly for in the past.

Never underestimate the power of a family with everything at stake.

Naomi cleared her throat. "Her name was Agnès. Robert's duchess was French, and he apparently loved her very much."

After having searched through the family records, Naomi had had the inspired idea to look in the small chapel at Monsale Castle. There at the bottom of the altar, she had discovered the name of the woman who had been the first duchess to swear the oath. A role that Monsale was proud to know his bride was more than ready to fulfil.

The prince gave a tired sigh. "I don't particularly care who she was, but you have to speak the words of the oath in Latin. Without that, all the McNeal family history becomes rather meaningless."

Monsale and Naomi exchanged a knowing look. "In the eyes of god and the law, man and wife are one body are they not?" he asked.

A bemused prince turned to his private secretary. The smile on the courtier's face was now gone, in its place was a look of deep concern. This was not going how either he or the prince had clearly hoped it would. "Yes, they are, marriage creates one person from the two. Your highness, it is a legal doctrine in England. The wife becomes the husband."

The Prince of Wales sighed. "Yes, though pity that my wife is still bound to me. Go on then."

With his heart full of pride, Monsale bowed his head while Naomi recited the words, she had carefully copied from the statue of Agnès McNeal.

"Promitto in fidem meam, quod ego in posterum fidelem, nunquam faciat ei malum, et mandata mea homagium ei omnino contra omnes homines, bona fide et sine dolo. In nomine patris, et filii, et spiritus sancti."

There was brief hush in the room, followed by the prince angrily summoning his advisors to gather their papers and follow him into an adjourning room. The courtiers scurried after the prince.

Monsale and Naomi remained where they were, kneeling on the floor. Neither dared to make a move. Loud shouts of 'bloody ridiculous' and 'why didn't you stop him getting married?' could be heard from the other room.

They both flinched as the door swung open and crashed against the wall. A fuming Prince of Wales stormed back into the throne room, followed by a procession of silent royal advisors.

He towered over Monsale. "I accept your oath of fealty, but just remember I shall hold you to it. And in the future when I call upon you to show me your loyalty, you will not hesitate."

"We are both sworn to serve you, your highness," replied Monsale, doing his best to keep his tone even and measured.

They had bested the future king, but neither he nor Naomi wished to make Prinny their enemy. The prince's pride had been badly bruised. This moment called for a strategic peace offering.

"As this is the anniversary of the swearing of the oath, my wife and I would be honored if you would accept a small token of our loyalty to the crown," said Monsale.

Adan stepped into the throne room, in his hands was the small treasure chest. Monsale helped his wife to her feet. He beckoned his steward to come forward. As Adan passed the box over, Monsale leaned in and whispered. "Thank you, my friend."

"It's the least I could do," replied Adan.

As Adan took his leave, Monsale caught the look of satisfaction on his loyal servant's face. It had taken quite some convincing for him to give up the coins. He had haggled hard on the bargain, something which Monsale was privately proud of him for having done.

In the end, the Spanish doubloons had been traded for a significant increase in Adan's shareholding of the RR Coaching Company.

Monsale turned and presented the prince with the chest. "A gift to celebrate this fine day, your highness."

Prinny eagerly took the box and opened it. The Spanish doubloons glinted in the morning sun; their brightness only matched by the smile on the prince's face.

"I thank you for your gift, Monsale, and I accept your fealty. You and your wife may leave."

He barely acknowledged Monsale's bow, or Naomi's curtsy as he stuffed his hand into the chest and let the coins run through his fingers.

Once he and Naomi were outside and, in the courtyard, Monsale nodded to her.

"You were right. He fully expected me to trip up with the language. And if you hadn't thought that might be the case, I could be standing here right now, plain old Mister Andrew McNeal."

She smiled sweetly at him. "You my love, will never be anything plain. Now let us go home; and while you are peeling this gown off my body, you can tell me how fortunate a man you are to have me as your duchess."

Monsale raised Naomi's hand to his lips. "Did I mention that a new shipment of yellow roses was arriving this morning? I suggest we adjourn to the hot house, so I may show you them."

Desire flashed in her eyes. "Yellow roses. That's new. I was thinking that perhaps you and I should swear our own oath. One which involves us having to find a different way to reach our climax whenever you take delivery of a new shade of flower. We could begin as soon as we get home."

Monsale raised an eyebrow. "I must warn you, that there are at least twenty-four variations of color for roses. This could become interesting."

They left Carlton House without delay.

Epilogue

"I can't believe we are actually here," said Bridget. She and Alice both giggled. Naomi shook her head. Her friends were behaving like young girls making their social debut, but she could understand their eager excitement. The first time she had set foot inside Monsale House, had also been surreal.

Until their recent marriage her husband had kept the place closed to all but a handful of friends. He was still reluctant to have guests, but to his credit Monsale was trying to change. This evening they were hosting their wedding ball, and shortly Monsale House would be filled with hundreds of guests.

"I hope to be able to host ladies luncheons and afternoon book clubs very soon. We are just waiting on the new wallpaper to arrive for the main drawing room," said Naomi.

Alice gave a mock gasp of surprise. "He is letting you redecorate? Oh, Naomi what have you got over poor Monsale that would make him do that?"

Jane tittered. "It must be very good or very wicked. I can't imagine him allowing you to make the slightest of alterations otherwise."

A grinning Naomi let her friends have their fun. She was fast learning that actions spoke louder than words.

You shall soon know just how wonderful a man my husband is; how much he cares for his family, his friends.

She led them from the foyer and upstairs into the grand dining room. Monsale and the other members of the RR Coaching Company rose as the ladies entered the room. There were three other people present, Adan and the former stable hand Bob, along with Stephen's young brother Toby.

As the other women took their places next to their husbands, Naomi walked confidently to the head of the table. Once everyone was seated, she addressed the room.

"My lords, ladies, and valued friends. Welcome to Monsale House. An extraordinary meeting of the RR Coaching Company was conducted a short time ago, at which it was decided to liquidate the company. This meeting is to establish a new company, the RR Coaching and Railway Company."

"I've heard of railroads, they are wooden tracks, but what is a railway?" asked Jane.

Monsale got to his feet. "Railways are made of iron and will eventually replace railroads. They will also mean the end of the many coach services which travel up and down the country. In the north of England, there is already a proposal to expand the Stockton to Darlington tramway and make it into a railway. While the tramways currently move stock, there will come a time when they also carry passengers. Our company has made strategic investments in land as well as the metal bolts and materials that the people building and running those future railways are going to need."

He pointed a finger in the direction of his estate steward and former stable hand. "Adan and Bob have been invited to invest in the new company, and I am pleased to announce that they have both sensibly agreed. Master Toby Moore is also to receive a parcel of shares which will be held in trust by his brother Sir Stephen until Toby comes of age."

Lady Alice Steele got to her feet. "When you say we have made investments, what exactly do you mean? Where has the money come from?"

Monsale and Naomi exchanged a grin. They had been running a secret bet as to which of the wives would ask that particular question.

"Over the years, I have taken an extra cut of all the proceeds from the RR Coaching Company. And while some people assumed that it was to line my own pockets, it was, in fact, a form of savings. I've been preparing for the day when we all walked away from our…" He darted a glance at young Toby before continuing. "Previous business endeavors."

There were gasps and loud exclamations from the other wives, followed by a hubbub of chatter amongst the various couples. It took some time for the noise to finally die down, at the end of which Stephen got to his feet.

"It has also been agreed that we shall all hold our shares for the next five years. After that time, if anyone wishes to leave the company, Monsale will buy them out."

Naomi let out a small sigh of relief. Her husband had carried the weight of the new company for many years, it was only fair that the rest of their friends stand up and support him. And while she didn't enjoy the prospect of everyone else potentially walking away from the venture at some point in the future, she trusted Monsale's investment instincts.

One by one Harry, George, Gus, and Stephen all spoke. No one would be selling their shares. They all supported Monsale.

"If you can all please sign your names to the document of incorporation, then we can bring this meeting to a close," said Naomi.

She picked up a pen and signed her own name. While it wasn't legally binding for the women to sign, she and

Monsale were both keen to have everyone's name on the document. For everyone to agree.

Monsale then signed, as did the rest of those present. Even Toby carefully wrote his name. When the meeting was officially closed, everyone but Monsale and Naomi filed out of the room. Monsale took a hold of Naomi's hand. There was a glint of excitement in his eyes as he bent and kissed her.

"Business is over and done with, now it's time to celebrate. Come my love, we have a ballroom of guests waiting for us downstairs."

She gifted him with a warm, teasing smile. "Let us linger here for a minute or two. You have helped to create a secure financial future for our friends and their families. I just want you to know how proud I am of my husband."

He kissed her once more. "Thank you. Hearing you say that, means the world to me."

❧

This was a special night and Monsale was grateful that Naomi wanted them to be alone for a time before they were caught up in a whirl of people.

He took in the dark silver of her silk gown, enjoying the stunning way it hugged Naomi's curves. She was every inch a duchess. From the diamond tiara which glittered in her hair, to the emerald bracelet which adorned her wrist.

The look of joy on her face when he gave her the ornate jewels would forever be one of his happiest memories. He knew it wasn't the precious stones which had brought tears to her eyes, it was the knowledge that he now felt free enough of his past to share his heart with her. To openly gift her his love.

Naomi slipped her arms around his neck, pulling him down for a long, tempting kiss. Her fingers ruffled through his hair. "What foolish people invited five hundred guests to our home tonight? We could be enjoying the warmth of the hot house and those lavender roses which arrived this afternoon."

He gave a deep chuckle in response to the promise in her words. "Later my love. And don't you go getting me all hard before we have to go and greet your parents."

She mewled with disappointment. "Just remember our deal. New roses. New game."

"Tonight, I promise."

He led her out of the dining room, and to the top of the stairs where Adan was waiting, the Monsale staff in his hand. He bowed. "Are your graces ready?"

Monsale and Naomi both smiled. "Yes."

They followed him down to the doorway of the ballroom. It had been a major effort to empty the room of all the crates of roses, but Monsale didn't want to risk any of them being damaged.

From the ballroom came the hum of many voices. The chatter and laughter all ceased as Adan, rapped the staff on the floor and announced. "My lords, ladies, and gentlemen. The Duke and Duchess of Monsale."

Monsale led Naomi through the door and straight to the middle of the room. At his signal the sixty-piece orchestra struck up the opening notes of a waltz.

"Never forget, from this day forth all my dances are yours. As is my heart."

"I love you, Monsale."

There in front of all of London's elite, he drew Naomi into his embrace. This woman was his world. And tonight, he would show everyone just how much he loved her. How she had always been the one for him.

She let out a laugh, filled with such joy, that he almost missed his footing as he spun his bride into the first turn of the dance. But as it was always when he was with Naomi, Monsale quickly recovered.

Thank heavens you never put your name on that list.

The king of rogues finally had his queen.

If you want to meet up with the Rogues of the Road again, they feature in Devoted to the Spanish Duke.

A Spanish noblewoman, kidnapped and far from home, must place her trust in the hands of a man who is the bitter enemy of her family.

Lisandro de Aguirre, Duke of Tolosa has few enemies greater than the Elizondo family. A bitter feud has existed between the two clans for over a hundred years.

Maria de Elizondo Garza is stolen from her home and taken to London as a hostage. A king's ransom now demanded by her secret captors.

With hope fading fast, Maria's brother turns to the one man he knows who can save his sister, Lisandro de Aguirre.

But when her family's enemy arrives to rescue her, Maria is determined not to go quietly.

A battle of wills soon turns into a war against simmering desire. How can the man she has been taught to hate, be the one who holds her heart?

A dangerous journey home has Maria and Lisandro both resisting the growing attraction between them, but a night of steamy passion makes them finally face up to the truth.

Back in Spain, all is not what it would seem; and they are forced to face the hardest question of all.

Can you truly trust your enemy?

Devoted to the Spanish Duke

Wow-Wow Sauce

You didn't think I would include this in the book and not give you the recipe!

Ingredients.

- Handful of finely chopped parsley leaves.
- Chop 3-4 pickled cucumbers or pickled walnuts into small pieces.
- 1 large tablespoon of butter (about the size of an egg)
- Tablespoon of plain flour
- ½ pint of beef broth (1.25 cups)
- Tablespoon of vinegar
- Tablespoon of mushroom ketchup or port wine (or both)
- Teaspoon of fine mustard

Place in saucepan and simmer until it becomes thick. Then pour over roast beef.

From the original recipe by Dr. William Kitchener. The Cook's Oracle. Published 1817.

Love Audio Books ?

Click HERE to listen to the first chapter of all audio books by Sasha Cottman

Audio titles are available at all major retailers and lending libraries.

About the Author

USA Today bestselling author Sasha Cottman was born in England, but raised in Australia. Having her heart in two places has created a love for travel, which at last count was to over 55 countries. A travel guide is always on her pile of new books to read.

Sasha's novels are set around the Regency period in England, Scotland, and Europe. Her books are centred on the themes of love, honour, and family. Visit her website at www.sashacottman.com

For international editions of novels, please visit www.sashacottman.com

Printed in Great Britain
by Amazon

57129839R00121